MW00366235

The Lavender Boys
and Elsie

Also by Tommy Womack

BOOKS

The Lavender Boys & Elsie

Cheese Chronicles: The True Story of a
Rock and Roll Band You've Never Heard Of
(Eggman Publishing, 1995)

MUSIC

There, I Said It!
(Cedar Creek Music / Thirty Tigers Dist., 2007)

Daddy At The Womens' Club (with Will Kimbrough)
(Cedar Creek Music, 2005)

Washington DC
(Cedar Creek Music, 2003)

Circus Town
(Sideburn Records, 2002)

Stubborn
(Sideburn Records, 2000)

Positively Na Na
(Checkered Past Records, 1998)

It's a Rock and Roll Party With Government Cheese
(Self-release single, 1995)

the bis-quits
(Oh Boy! Records, 1993)

Government Cheese
(LAR Music, 1992)

Three Chords No Waiting (with Government Cheese)
(Reptile Records, 1989)

C'mon Back to Bowling Green . . . And Marry Me
(with Government Cheese)
(Reptile Records, 1987)

Things Are More Like They Are Now Than
They've Ever Been Before (with Government Cheese)
(Our Records, 1985)

The Lavender Boys

and *Elsie*

Tommy Womack

Copyright ©2008 by Tommy Womack

All rights reserved. Unathorized duplication is a violation of applicable laws.

This work was previously archived as an online novella on tommywomack.com and printed once before in a limited edition of 50 copies.

First commercial edition: 2008

ISBN-13: 978-0-9818867-0-1
ISBN-10: 0-9818867-01

Mary Sack Management
P.O. Box 330911
Nashville, Tennessee
37203-7506

http://www.tommywomack.com
http://www.myspace.com/tommywomack
http://www.cedarcreekmusic.com

The characters in this book, despite the author's best attempts to make the reader think otherwise, are fictitious. Any resemblance to any persons, living or dead, is entirely coincidental.

Interior Design by Keata Brewer
Cover Design by Brad Talbott

For Mom, Beth, Nathan,
and gay soldiers everywhere

Copious thanks to
Richard Courtney, Maryglenn McCombs, Mary Sack,
Keata Brewer, Brad Talbott, Eddie's Attic,
Ann Witzany and Paula Millen for all their help
and guidance in getting this story told.

Introduction

As a Civil War buff, I've long heard whispered tales of The Lavender Boys, that little Confederate regiment with a difference. Like most everyone else, I've always figured they were just that—tales. There is no record of any such regiment ever existing; but to conspiracy theorists, that proves more than it disproves.

They point to the numerous fires, many suspicious in origin, that have destroyed so many Confederate military records.

They point to a letter sent by a Mississippian Confederate Corporal, McKinley Daniel, in November, 1862, to his wife back home, that says, *"Those Lavinder Boys may be light on their feet, but they're ready for action when need be!"*

Then there's the letter from Private Elias Morganfield of Waycross, Georgia, to his mother, also from November, 1862, in which he writes *"Got a bunch of male nerses camp'd next to us now. All of um "that way". Sickning! But hell, thay can aim and shoot. Stick um up front I reckon!"*

Confederate Vice-President Alexander Stephens in January, 1863 wrote to his wife, bemoaning Southern shortages of all goods: from coffee and sugar, to gunpowder and manpower. Of the latter, *"It's come to this, dearest—arming queers! Next I fear it will be the slaves!"*

Lavender Boys theorists point most of all, to an unsigned memo marked "TOP SECRET. For Gen'l R. E.

Lee ONLY. June 27th, 1863". It was discovered in a hidden wall safe, among Lee's most private papers, in 1928.

"As per private conversation, LB cancer must be removed with all speed and regardless of cost. Please act at once."

The handwriting matches that of Jefferson Davis, the date is six days prior to Pickett's Charge at Gettysburg, when Lee ordered General George Pickett's entire division—thousands of men—to march defenseless and exposed across an open field and into a solid wall of Yankee lead, cannon and mortar fire.

Southern losses were appalling that afternoon. Almost to a man, Pickett's entire division was left dead on the field, a sea of mangled humanity—with no strategic gain whatsoever.

For the brilliant Lee to have ordered such a senseless and suicidal charge has left historians scratching their heads ever since. For Lavender Boys conspiracy buffs, it explains everything. Lee, they say, was following Davis's orders to the letter, with all speed and regardless of cost. An entire division, they assert, was sacrificed, so that one regiment bunched within its ranks might disappear forever. Just as some people maintain that Roswell wasn't about a weather balloon, and others insist that Kennedy was shot from the grassy knoll, so people the world over remain convinced that Robert E. Lee did just such a thing—sending thousands of good men to their deaths just to camouflage all knowledge of some gay men in grey.

In the autumn of 1996, I was living in Nashville, as I still do now, and had been a musician of local renown for a decade or more. The year before, my book *Cheese Chronicles*, about life in a rock and roll band, had made me a minor celebrity in town, more so than my music ever had. I got invited to a lot of cocktail parties for a while, and a lot of book signings. One of those signings was in Franklin, a town south of Nashville full of charming shops, small-town flavor and folks with more money than God. The Civil War, as in The Battle of Franklin—ran right through town and don't you forget it.

The book signing was for a local author who'd just produced a Civil War-era historical novel. Present were a mélange of socialites, a couple of Country and Christian music stars, and—to everyone's barely contained excitement—a very famous Hollywood actor. I was introduced to him and found myself utterly tongue-tied, which is rare for me. I was trying to get out the words "Nice to meet you" and failing, when he grabbed my hand, looked me in the eye and said "I love your book." I was flabbergasted! HE knew who *I* was! I was on Cloud Nine the rest of the night, especially since this very famous actor seemed more interested in talking to me than to most anyone else. We talked mainly about Civil War matters as I discovered his interests matched mine there, and that he was an ardent collector of uniforms, weapons and artifacts. When he asked me if I believed the Lavender Boys existed, I said no. Preposterous on its face, I said. He just smiled. We talked about politics (and our left-of-center commonalities thereof), music, anything but his movies. It was a great night. I figured I'd never meet him again but could always say I had.

Six months later the phone rang. It was the actor. He had a proposition. Would I take a $1000 advance to come to Los Angeles, transcribe some 1860s correspondence with aims toward making it a movie script. I asked what the correspondence was and was told that I would find that out in Los Angeles.

So I flew to L.A. and was taken by limousine to the actor's home in Beverly Hills. The actor wasn't there. I was met at the door by a very fat Asian personal assistant who spoke thickly accented English and sported a moustache and kimono. I was sat down in a study and in short order handed a drink and a contract to sign. The contract had nothing to do with any script, but was rather an agreement not to disclose anything I saw or heard while under the employ of said actor. I said I wasn't signing dick until I saw my money. I was then shown a check for $500, which the kimono guy kept in his hand. I said I was supposed to get a thousand. He said I'd get the first half now and the rest when the typing was done. By now I was weirded-out a little. Can't they get anybody to type up some old letters?

I asked the fat dude why me? He said, gruffly "Taro say man who type letters then type script, then we all make big money!" and he slapped his belly to emphasis the money part. I saw what money meant to him, the 24-ounce ribeye at Outback! "Boss say you good writer, you type letters, you type script."

"Who's Taro?" I asked.

"TARO!" he shouted, pointing to the palm of one hand, "Card!"

Oh, ahh, tarot cards. I see. The tarot cards say he who types the letters gets to write the script. This was looney.

But hell, I needed the money, I signed.

I was then shown the 47 documents that make up this

book—42 letters, 3 telegrams, one postcard and an obituary notice. Each yellowed sheet of paper was sheathed in its own protective cellophane and held in a three-ring binder. I was also shown—without asking for it—three independent forensic test results all dating the ink and the paper to the 1860s.

I looked over the first few pages and my blood ran cold. These were letters between a brother and a sister, Albert and Elsie Devereaux. I'd never heard of Elsie, but I knew all too well who Albert Devereaux was supposed to have been. You see, just as the Lavender Boys never really existed (if you believe that way); neither did their mythical Captain, Albert Devereaux!

He appears in no official war records whatsoever. And yet here I was reading letters from him, describing his life in a Civil War camp, arguing with his sister about his sexuality, recording his experiences in battle. My heart nearly came out of my chest. This was bombshell stuff, and it wasn't going to make me any friends at re-enactments!

For eight hours a day the next seven days, I typed up those letters in the actor's own study. I was never allowed to be alone with the letters. A private security guard stared a hole in me the whole time every day. I typed the documents directly onto a floppy disc which I handed to the guard at the end of every session. (Yes, we still used floppies back then.) He leaned against the wall facing me, standing by the computer. He really thought he was a smart cookie. Trouble is, from his angle he could see me fine but couldn't see the computer screen at all, thus not noticing how every ten minutes or so I copy-pasted everything and saved it to a folder on the hard drive called

"Recipes", which I later e-mailed to myself, which is the only reason you now have this book in your hands today.

It didn't take me long to figure out what the non-disclosure agreement was all about. I saw the actor come and go (and he was much less friendly now that I was his employee), but I never saw his famous actress wife nor any evidence she even lived there. There wasn't even a picture of them together on a wall. I noticed how all the housekeeping staff seemed to be scared stiff and dared not even say hello, and I heard the kimono guy on the phone quite a lot, making deals, donating money. I overheard enough to figure out that this famous actor was very active behind the scenes in gay and lesbian causes, mainly because he was very active behind the scenes in being gay.

Among other things, I heard the kimono guy on the phone saying "You know we switch publicists . . . Boss is coming out . . . all the way out! . . . Sure, shit hit fan, but we have great project in works . . . we own all rights . . . have writer typing big hit out right now."

So the actor was "coming out"! *I get it now!* He's going to come out and have in his pocket a big-budget gay-themed Civil War blockbuster, and I was gonna write the script! And for surely more than $1000. Holy shit, I thought, I'm gonna be rich!

Once I'd typed all the letters, and handed the floppy to the guard for the last time, I packed my bags and called my own cab. I was ready to go home. I don't mind gay scenes, but this place was a house of freaks. I went looking for the kimono guy to pick up the other half of my $1000. He said he'd send it in the mail to me. We got in a shouting match and I was ejected from the property by an armed guard. I got in my cab and split. That was eleven years ago.

The actor never did switch publicists, never has come out of the closet, and he still owes me $500.

I tried to do things the right way. For years! I called and called and have never gotten a call back. I've written letters that were never responded to—all to no avail. Then I got mad.

I figured if he reneged on his payment to me, I was no longer obligated to live up to his non-disclosure agreement. So I decided to go ahead and publish these letters myself, for the sake of history, for the sake of the Lavender Boys. I'd tell you the actor's name but he'd sue me 'til there wasn't a scrap on my bones. The best I can hope for is that I'll prick his paranoia to the point that he'll quietly relinquish the original documents to a museum or library or some venue where their existence can be verified. Until then, I can't prove a thing. You can say I just made up this whole business. But I didn't. The Lavender Boys were real. You'll just have to take my word for it. For now.

Read on. Enjoy the shocking true story of the Lavender Boys. And on a side note, if any detectives in the Clarksville, Tennessee area are working cold murder cases over a century old—these letters might clear up a few things there too.

Tommy Womack
August 2008

The Lavender Boys
and Elsie

September 23rd, 1861

My Dear Sister;

A million thanks for the jam cake! Nothing tastes of
home like your jam cake! And THIS time none of the
roughies made off with any. I showed them! This time I
pick'd up your pkg, went straightaway off behind a tree
and ate the whole thing all at once, and that's quite a lot
of jam cake. I strolled on back into camp all stuff'd and
bloated, full of sugar humor, and the worst roughie
Harrison was smoking a pipe in front of his tent. He
call'd out "Hey Dev'ro! What'd yer sister send us?" I
holler'd back "She ain't sent nothing I ain't already et!"
whilst keeping walking and not turning around to see if
he was mad. I spent that evening and much of the next
day near the latrine, never quite vomiting but often
thinking I was just about to.

It would have been nice to have just had a piece to
eat per evening as my dessert every night for however
long it lasted, but that's a little more than can be
expected here in the seat of all that is most vile, so I just
sat behind that tree and ate it all in one rush of
engorgement! Really! I was shoveling berries and syrup
and cake down my gullet like a bear racing winter and it
tasted so like home that for a while there I was, looking
off the trace with the corn all put up and the breeze just
getting cool and autumnal for the first time and I was
home. The berries brought me home.

I trust Stepfather is well. Does he speak of me? I
reckon not most likely, but what I said is what I said and

that is that. Give my best to the others and see if they know what to do with it. Ha!

You should do your best to keep them in your prayers, dear Sister, and I know how hard that can be. I know they're hard on you but don't harden your own heart back They're just dumb is all. They don't mean half of what they say to you and you take it all to heart way harder than they sling it. It's never folks' fault being stupid. They just are, I suppose. They can't help it. Nobody gets up in the morning and says oh boy I'm going to be dumb as wood today and boy won't it get folks' goats 'cause I'll say such rotten meanness and won't ever know it 'cause I'm an unthinking pile of horse gush such as the Lord has determined there needs to be so much of. No. If they weren't so dumb then maybe they'd realize how stupid they are and then they'd do something about it or at least try. But stupid people always tend to think they're pretty smart—that's the worst thing about them. They think they're where they need to be, and they're all happy about it. Such are the ways of the Lord.

So we have now exchanged two complete rounds of correspondence and not a WORD about my confession! You're the only person I have entrusted this knowledge unto and such silence for a reply leaves me no more satisfied than had I bared my soul to a tree. Do you have anything to say?! I mean, I wasn't joking, no light-making japery, I'm serious. I'm positive this time.

I promise to write more (and soon) but I'm tuckered. It's ten o- clock now, reveille is five-thirty, and I want to drop this in the box before I fall fully out.

Tommy Womack

I love you and I miss you and don't you worry anymore about me, I know that last letter came soaked in pitiable tears but never mind that, I'm doing better all the time. All this is making a man out of me (or as close as I'll may ever likely feel to being such). I do miss home madly, to be sure, the piano and the reading Dickens aloud, getting the Harper's on time. Here it's endless drilling and sleeping outdoors and the bugs, the bugs, THE BUGS! BIG bugs like you've never seen before! Alabama bugs!

But this IS "The Big Show" as they say. I could look forward to telling my grandchildren about it someday but you know how likely THAT is now. Ha! I've at least stopped trying to pin down exactly what in samhill I must have been thinking coming down here to muster up to begin with!, as there's no use asking when it makes no difference anymore, is there? Because here I be! For eighteen more months! And there's this one Sargeant who's always going around laughing and saying 'once they got you, they got you as long as they wawnt you, son!' (Aye!)

Those first Coffee County yahoos who worked me over a bit are gone now and good riddance. They went off to defend some coastal battery and no doubt terrorize the locals and ravage their women. Since then, most of the others have actually been quite nice, really. They're all such country boys, hardly a one ever been away from home before. We're all scared and lonely in our own ways, I guess. They don't notice anymore that I'm not 'from Alabam' and they're not always inquiring about my accent and asking why didn't you muster where yer from boy? and stuff like that. I'm just kind-of one of the fellows. Ha!

I worry more for YOU, dear sister. You're fragile and you let them bother you so. Your mind sets to conjuring things that aren't there. Really! Thoughts of murder! I can't ever think any of them are out to DO YOU IN like you think, my dear. They're just stupid is all. Stupid and mean. None of them are smart enough to do murder. You're smarter than they are! Just don't let their practical jokes and jibes get to you so! Besides, why would they kill you? Who'd do the wash then? Ha!

Write soon. We're still in Montgomery, but so long as you get the battalion and regiment numbers right on the envelope, it should get to me directly enough, wherever we go.

Your loving brother,
Albert

My dear Albert;

*How it tares at my heart to read of you getting mistreeted so
by those other boys! Don't you eat that much jam cake at once
like that again! I do not bake things so as to they're suppos'd
to be et all at once like that! You're lucky your insides don't
twist up like a horse's! You stay away from all those bullys,
Albert, and don't you take up their sinnful ways. Stay away
from the cards and the drinking. You read your Bible and
your Shakesperre. What of those other boys know their
Shakesperre, and play the piano and sing like a bird what
other boys have your pretty face? (thankyu for the tintype! So
handsom!) Your face is so soft like our Mother's. Her eyes are
yors and I can see it more clearly then er' b'fore. So like two
perls taking in the world. She was too good for this world,
too tender and true. You're too good for that world you're in
down ther too. Do not consort with scoundrels. You are my
sweet boy I did my best to raise you like Mother would have
approved of and you make such a handsom soldier. Now God
hold you as I entreet him dayly to and I'm sure you do as
well.*

*I am afrad for my spelling as without you here to learn
me it goes right out of my head. I never took to it like
you,(but thank you for saying I'm smarter than them. Ha!)
yr right about the wash! And believe me I do plenty of that
around here. I guess you'r right, brother, they'd be doing off
with the hand that cleans up after them.*

*But they really DO hate me, though, Albert! It's not just
that they're stupid though I reckon it's true they may well be.
(Smart as you are, if you think I'm smarter than them thats
good enough for me and I just say thankyu, Albert, so you go*

on ahead and kep saying that in every letter ha!.) But I'm not "conjuring" things such as you say. Yesterday Melanie smeared lard grease on my bedroom doorknob and giggled as she run'd off. I know her laugh and I know the sound of her shoes clomping around and I know it was her. AND I know Stepfather won't do a thing to her. He won't make either one of those girls help me keep this house clean wirth a wick. But I cannot go on TOO harshly about Bart Jr. right now because he is across the table from me this instant, and I am not lying, he is WRITING YOU A LETTER TOO! Right now! Isn't that wonderful??!! I've been begging this whole family to write you and send you love and prayers and strength and now at least one of them is! Bad as it may be, family is family, and stepfamily's worse, but when it's all you've got it's all you've got.

Stepfather continues down his footsurre path toward being the worst thing ever could've walked and I'm sorry as I can be to say that I'm praying every day on it believe me! He's not spoken of you, I'm sorry to say. he just prowls the place day and night always so distracted that I used to wonder sometimes if he realizes yu're gone at all, but yu been gone so long now he HAS to know. He has been all wrap't up in setting up his legal affairs. This last consumption put his own mortal life up front in his head, I think. He has the lawyer Hanks in from town over to the house oft'n and they go over deeds and stock papers and what appears to be the will. (Not being blood, I wonder how we're to be remember'd such, Lord forgiv'me, knowing how sinful and greedy to think about such things of a man who's not dead tho Lord knows how I'v prayed for him to be sometimes!)

I shouldn't write such things becawse I already feel so

fearful in this house. The hate here! At night I hear Bart and
his sisters talk, talk, talk, talk about the will, and their
father's health, and they talk about us and they talk about
Mother and about how she brought collera into this house
like she meant to or something like that, I don't know!
THAT's crazy, brother! I'M not the insane case here.
THAT is crazy! What THEY speak of at night, in their
rooms, whilst I struggle to hear in my little humble bedsit
downstairs off the kitchen, listening to the ceiling in night
after night in MY DANK CORNER DAMP struggling to
make out THEIR TRECH'RUS WORDS and intents.

Your stepsisters are fighting again upstairs right now!
Over a bonnet I think. I hear their hard leather soles
scuff on the floor of their bedroom upstairs. You wouldn't
think they're eighteen and sixteen, the way they squabble
like four-year-olds.

It looks like it may sqwall and I don't want the wash to
get all wet. Please write me soon, my BRAVE SOLDIER.

Enclosed is something what come in yesterday to Baxter's
he says he's alreddy having trouble filling some orders because
of the blockade, but this came. Be careful putting your hand
in. There's a razor down there!

Your loving sister ever,
Elsie

17th OCT., '61

PS
Regarding your confession. I'm sorry if I've appeared
reluctant to address the situation but I reckon I have been.

I'v herd this same song out yur mouth since yu were 13 and I've always taken it to the Lord and trusted how someday you'll just come to realize you don't really feel this way. Dear heart, yu'wre a confus'd and lonely young boy in a bad home and now yu're a confus'd and lonely young man—and to be in a soldier's camp on top of it! You're hard on yourself like I think happens when a boy comes of age not where he's from. To be a fullblood French Cajun in Clarksville, Tennessee far and away from blood kin and their ways didn't do neither one of us any favors ha! But God takes care of that in time for each and all creatures great and small according to his own Will and Judgement God don't come when you call Him but he's always on time! And when God decides it's time for you to discover the right woman to gladden your heart then you'll find her that day and fall right in love and it'll be His will and no way other. You just have to be patient. Besides that, I just don't think it's possible. I don't think there's such thing as homosexuals anymore than I think there's really vampyres and trolls! Love you, E

Dear Fagget;

In order to shut your sister up I am taking the time to rite you a letter She is I loking at me as I rite this and is so proud for me doing so i hope she dasnt see how I'm really just ritting to get her off my head and tell you the TRUTH and the TRUTH is you'r going to get your HEdD BLOUD' OFF and if not by some Yanky then by one of our own proud and real REBELL MEN thinning the GOD-damned out THE HERD and weren't I not slowd' down so with consumption and such you bet your ASS I'd be THERE ON THE FRONT LINE so dont think your so brave and Big Man because your not look at her smile at me and so proud like I have turned a corner over you No sir you make me sick! rememmber you can't shoot straight with a dick in your mouth Go off and try and prove you're some kind of real man cause you're a GOD-Dammed QUEERr and I'm not taking the LORDS NAME in vain because HE damns you HIMSELF in the BIBLE and damn anybody else who DON'T damn you and by the way I know how you talked to my Daddy in the street that last day and you just best be glad yur gone now and it also just shows how much you know about the man he fought in Mexico under ZACK TAYLOR and he's kilt more men then you wil because the Army's going to snif you out and kick your ass out because they dont alow your kind, Albert Canjunfagget. Go on

Bartholomew Jansch the II.

October 30th, 1861

Dearest kind sister Elsie;

Vampyres and trolls of all things! I must say that your own PS of last has left me feeling utterly alone. I've always felt quite alone in this affair and now moreso. I was hoping you'd have more belief in me. How ironic that I spend so much time trying to convince you that how you see things isn't how they are and then you turn around and tell me that my own heart and desires as I know them to be is some sort of misdiagnosis or a phase I'll grow out of like youthful blemishes. Dear, homosexuals exist as surely as beech elms and starlings do. I'm in full contact with what I know of love and attraction and feelings in my heart. I've wandered the road into town and back enough times to circle the globe, I've THOUGHT about this with great pains at length. And how I feel is very real, sister. Please understand, I need you to know that. We're all each other has and this is now a chasm that wounds my soul.

That aside, you astound me! What prescient giftliness! A proper shaving kit is an answer to prayers! I feel human again, all stropped and close-shaved and pomaded and fussed up for the first time in a while. You'd almost think I haven't been sleeping out in the open air the last six weeks!

You might not know me anyway! I am dark red as if it were full summer still. There is a thickness and squareness to me now that I've never had before and believe me when I tell you I've been earning it. I thought I knew what vigorous outdoor behavior was, dear sister—as a fellow in my unit says, I knew Jack Shit (and that means I knew nothing in Army slang). At night when I crumple to the ground under my tent-half and my aching muscles tell me again and again everything Sergeant Major had me do all day. They afford me an excellent opiated contentment that is total and pure fatigue. Sergeant Major ferrets out any and all unspent energy in some backbreaking task before each day is done. Every night now I lie under my tent-half, stars above my head, and I can be so ironically satisfied because I am too deep tired to muster any disgruntlement, ponder any problem or nurse a bad notion. There's so many other fellows laying in the same grass across these great fields that I feel like everyone can hear my thoughts drifiting across the nighttime sky anyway. Besides! I sleepwalk! What if I confess in my sleep! (That could REALLY be bad around here! Ha! small nervous ha)

When I say Sergeant Major, I don't mean that's his rank, and this is the source of much jocularity and confusion. He is Franklin Major, a Baptist minister from Tuscaloosa and being our Sergeant he is thusly Sergeant Major, you see, and WORN OUT on the jokes. It's quite funny to see a higher-ranking officer make a pun of it and Sgt. Major will be all smiley kissa—like it's not the thousandth time someone's cracked every variation on the wise wise remark about it—but woe unto the LOWLIER SOUL who should make foolish idle jest! Sargeant Major is a large man. Very large. Big belly, big moustache, a bigger voice than all outdoors. He and I have had a very simple relationship—he hollers, I do. But unlike some other fellows who've given me ponted grief, Sgt. Major doesn't seem to see much difference between me and any other soldier, he treats us all the same—we all get the same holler'd speeches full of scripture and Old Testament admonitions of battle and otherwise get treated like dogs.

And when I say I sleep under a tent-half I mean I live underneath my tent-HALF! We all got one half of a tent (six weeks ago) and it's up to our own intitiavtive to find a nighttime companion so as to make tent and sleep with a much better expectation of not waking soaked, chilled, covered with dry leaves or ashes, or manure, or anything else drifting by in the wind. Anyway, the day they were issued, I got suddenly called away by Corporal Rawley who really has it in for me. (I'm "Kansas City Boy" to him.) He sent me on a bullshine snipe-hunt just as the wagon arrived, so when that I returned there was one tent-half left on the ground and all 148 other men of my company had their tents put together already. That left me odd man out, number 149, the Kansas City Boy. That was six weeks ago and I'm STILL odd-out 149. I assure you dear, it is NOT all in my head! I know you've heard this story since I was 13, that's because it's a TRUE STORY, It's MINE, and I need you. Please believe me, dear sister. I'm sleeping under the open sky with a canvas rectangle barely larger than I am. I have NO FRIENDS. I need you to believe me!

Once again I apologize for such a short letter. I know you're dying for details of what my life is like in the

Tommy Womack

camp, and I'll do my best to satisfying that curiosity forthwith. I promise that. BUT right now I want to scribble a few lines of thanks to Bart for his own kind letter. (He wrote me!!!! Just like you said! How thrilling!) I'll write more later. Trust in God to relieve you of your sad fortune in life, our sad fortune as family, and all sad things you must endure. I remember you always in all my own missives to the Almighty. I love you always.

Yours ever,
Albert

PS
Vampyres and trolls! Really! Is it that hard to believe the coniditon exists in our natural diemension as beings? As animals with natures? It happens! Just ask Bart! Love, A

Dear Imbecile;

COULD THIS BE YOU? My compliments on your SPELING.

I mentioned you to Sergeant Major today (not a Sergeant-Major but . . . no never mind . . .) that you missed regimental muster up in Tennessee because of consumption. Oh did he laugh. "Haw!" he says "CONSUMPTION kep him out of the big show? Hell I'd rather folks think I's QUEER than kep down of consumption."

He walked away from me still laughing, then he came back. "Wuzzat consumption boy's name?" and I said "Bartholomew Jansch the Second, of Clarksville, Tennessee." and so then he walked away apparently content that it was at least no one he knew. Well, that's all from the manly front of warfare. Do take care of the womenfolk and try and remember to come inside when it rains.

Best wishes always,
Albert the Fagg

November 1st, 1861

My dear sister Elsie;

True to my word I'm writing more now. It is just an
evening or two later and I'm my usual tired as tired can
be. You'd not believe how much they can make you do
in one day, let you sleep a little bit and then get you up
to do some more. And to think we haven't even gotten
around to any FIGHTING yet.

Fighting! The very thought makes me tighten up
inside like a corkscrew going up my back. The way they
make us work, I'm afraid I'll be too tired to fight when
that time comes.

Reveille generally comes about three seconds after I
lay my head down upon my haversack at night. One
second it's the evening and suddenly it's dawn. Clammy
and disoriented (and colder every passing morning!), I
spring up from the ground and am on my feet saying
things like "Yes Sergeant!" and "right away Sergeant!"
before I even know what I'm talking about.

We gather on a little clearing of ground in front of
where we sleep and we stand there in a line for roll call,
trying desperately not to yawn. A yawn is a demerit and
three demerits is latrine detail and you don't even want
to hear any about that. That's the first thing of the day,
we stand there presenting our rifles across our right
shoulders and facing straight ahead and Sergeant Major
goes down the roll. Whenever he gets to "Devereaux,
Albert, Private!" I endeavor to say "here!" in my most
basso profundo timbre.

Then we drill for a half hour. Drilling consists of marching this way and then that way and then this way again, occasionally stopping, occasionally turning around, occasionally forming into two lines with the ones of us in front on our knees and the ones in back standing erect and then we practice loading our weapons, raising and firing.

Oh my goodness, Elsie! That first CRACKETTYTACK of the morning! When all those guns go off at once?! You've never heard such noise! And the smoke and the smell! Then we all stand in the cloud of our own making and bite open a new bag of black powder and pour it into the barrel and ram it down and ram a little lead ball down and listen to the Sargeant's orders and we always keep trying to maintain our stance of disaffected manliness amongst it all, like we're not bothered or startled by the concussions, or the way the gun stocks kick back into our shoulders and the smoke stings all our eyes Truth is it's all about enough to make you wet your pants! It's obviously no business for rushing and yet a frenetic velocity is exactly what they want us to achieve. It hits me in those moments that the only thing concievably worse than being behind all this folderol and flying lead is of course the unsettling prospect of being in front of it all, and that one day soon I might find myself facing another line of men all with as much intentions of shooting me as I have of shooting them, and it disturbs me to think too long on it so I try not to, but the thought is not avoidable, especially in that moment when all our guns go off for the first time each morning. Every morning it's like I've never heard guns before and it's a shock to the system anew.

After that is breakfast and we're always mad ready for it. A Negro woman named Wenna cooks all day long for the entire regiment. She lives in a covered wagon and cooks the most excellent black eyed peas with ham, and it's a good thing she cooks them well because we have those black eyed peas and that ham every day! She speaks with such a delightful accent that makes me feel like a child when I hear it. She's from home! New Orleans!

But we are not friends. I don't think Wenna likes any of us. She's not a happy-go-lucky rapscallions negro, not that at all! Her features are iron-black, she dollops the food into our plates and bowls with an iron face like an Oriental warrior who knows all, feels nothing and gives no man the satisfaction of seeing whatever pain or happiness is inside. She is a huge woman. I'd never want to make her mad. Her right arm alone probably weighs what I do. I am intrigued with her because I cannot deduce whether she is happy, unhappy, or even if she world deduce a relevant difference between the two.

Breakfast is usually a bit of bacon, (not much, and not as good as yours!), some hominy and corn bread (two hunks to a man). Complain about your portion and she curses you with a thick accent that reminds me of being in New Orleans as such a wee lad all those years ago. Mother sounded like that. I like to imagine Father did as well.

It seems like every other day is a five to ten mile hike which at first was torture and now just feels merely bad. We have to ear all we own and carry our weapon and amunition. Enlisted man cannot carry extra belongings other than which can be affixed to his person somehow. Officers are allowed one trunk of stuff on supply wagons. (Commanding officers can apparently do whatever they want wherever they want and often do!) We're often told on seconds' notice to pack up all our belongings (including my splendid new shaving kit!), put them on our backs however we can manage, and march. If your pack falls apart on your back you fall out of formation, you pick it all up and run and catch up, or you lose your stuff, either way you'll be subjected to a torrent of abuse from Sergeant Major and the other lads, who all love to see someone made sport of, and I'll admit I feel a bit of relief and solidarity when the one being made fun of is occasionally not me.

I know you want to know more details about my day but it would numb you in the end, dear Elsie. It numbs me. It's all more of the same: drilling, cornbread, black-eyed peas, more drilling, hiking, guard duties, more cornbread, cast-iron coffee. My body is coming around to it. My mind, so alone and restive, is at least pacified by exhaustion. I wish I had a friend, though, someone nice who didn't revile me and think me too delicate to be seen with, someone I could share my thoughts with, a chewing gum, and your jam cake!

I was in "chow line" waiting to get my dollop from Wenna. We usually line up two abreast and march down both sides of her wagon with our plates held aloft. As often as not the fellow 'cross of us is from another company and Wenna will splash some food from her ladle into your plate, then into his, you go sit back in your camp and he goes to his. Well, today I found myself standing across from the most extraordinarily handsome man. Such eyes, Elsie!

You say I have our Mother's pearl eyes, well the deepest blue-white pearls have I looked into now and I know not his name. This handsome Private had my stare locked upon him, and he couldn't have not noticed, but where I so often get glares of menace in exchange, catcalls and threats, not today. He looked back at me and smiled! I smiled back. We didn't speak. But a smile dear sister! A smile after six weeks in this army camp is like a long drink of ice water from a clean glass!

He has a fair face and hair like a Dutchman's, from what I know of Dutch people. He has pretty front teeth and none too yellow nor broken up such as I could see when he smiled at me, and very high cheekbones with shadows underneath them, not like he was underfed and hollow, but sculpted and highbrow looking. We wound up almost side by side and Wenna ladled our plates close enough together to feel a slight bit of oneness about it. Perhaps I'll see him again.

It is late, dear sister. I pray that everything is fine at home, that the winter planting is done and the stock are all fine, that Melanie, Darcy and Bartholomew Jr. are all fine. (Thank him again for me for his nice letter!) And I hope that Stepfather is fine too. Has he said a word of me yet? Are you SURE he's noticed I'm gone? Ha!

Write soon!

All my love,
Albert

My dear Brother;

Whatever you wrote in your letter to Bart Jr. sure put the fire in his belly! And boy is Stepfather upset now because guess what!? Jr. has gone off to join the fight! That's right! He left yesterday morning with just a note on the table saying "I AM GONE TO THE WARR!" and was out of the house before sunup. You must have inspired his patriotism somehow.

But Stepfather is not pleased. He says he'll never see his dear son again. I asked him what about his other son and he said he didn't have any other son. He wanted to say he just had two daughters and not three, but he didn't. I could tell he wanted to though.

I hate to pass on things like that but you said you wanted me to be honest about what he says about you and that's what he said, that's about all he's mentioned of you either.

I'm sorry, dear Albert. I wish he'd show more love to you. I just KNOW he wishes we were both just wiped off the earth, like we were never here. Makes me nervous to be around him. If I had some where else to go live, I'd go there but I don't.

And I'm sorry if how I feel makes you feel alone about yourself. If you say there's homosexuals in the world, well and fine, but I've never seen one and I'm not of a mind to just throw up my hands and say well my little brother's embraced a perversion that'll take him straight to Hell. I'm sorry but I love you a little TOO MUCH for that.

Darcy and Melanie are going to a Confederate bond-raising ball in Clarksville tomorrow night. They insist I must fit and refit their dresses over and over. They never asked if I'd like to go with them. They don't know how I listen to them in their room at night, and how when they bring their voices down to a murmur I can hear them all the better, and how they're going to just keep me in the basement as their own charwoman when Stepfather dies!

They just take it for granted that my place is in this house, cooking the meals and looking after them and their father. They think I don't care any whit to go off to any silly ball, so they don't ask. They all just hate me.

Enclosed please find some cocoa ladyfingers. I've double-wrapped them in wax paper and they shouldn't bleed through the package like last time. I hope you enjoy them and have friends soon to share them with instead of bullies who just take them.

I can't write long because Father wants his boiled turkey and coffee and the girls are upstairs hollering for something, probably one of their hems aren't right. Melanie says any mistakes and I'm sleeping in the smokehouse. Then they laugh. Is that what you call teasing, Albert? They aren't teasing. Those girls would just as soon see my hams cut loose and smoking in the timbers, wherefrom I can't get my mitts on their father's loot, isn't that right?

Stepfather promised our mother on her deathbed he'd look after us and I suppose to his thinking he's done such. I have a bed with a roof over it, and while it's not as grand as the other girls have, it's not out in the stable either. Yu'r too young to remember, but I had high hopes as a young girl, gorwing up in New Orleans, and then the collera came and it took Daddy just like it took the first Mrs. Jansch. The ways of God are not for small minds to wigglyniggly over. It's a shame it was not your fate to grow to manhood in

---

The Lavender Boys and Elsie

Louisiana. You would have felt more at home there. Perhaps someday you'll come to know that grand city. They'd love your piano playing. And THERE I bet you'd find the right young lady.

I really must leave you now, but before I do let me tell you I know what Jack S—— is and shame on you! Such language! I warned you about consorting with scoundrels and here is the handiwork of their ways! Stepfather came through moaning right now, 'I can't believe Junior really left! Daft child!' Well he did, you might see him again before we do as I reckon he's off and mustered in a regiment already. I hope he does alright, he's not over the consumption, didn't look too well last I saw him and as you know he's none too bright.

All my love,
Elsie

10, NOV., '61

November 16, 1861

Dearest Sister Elsie;

What would my stomach do if not for you, my dear sister?! The ladyfingers are superb. They make the coffee we make here go down a little sweeter, AND YES, I have a friend with which to share them.

You see, I ran into that handsome young fellow in the chow line again. And again we both smiled at each other and we found a common bond in Shakespeare almost immediately, as if it were a gift from God for the right things to happen and give us a moment to look and acknowledge one another. We were right next to each other in Wenna's line and Major Hubble rode by. So under his breath some wag murmured "Hubble, Hubble . . ." and both Jorge and I simultaneously murmured back ". . . toil and trouble." and we then just looked right at each other and laughed. I love that first magic moment with someone you don't know yet and you're both as immaculate as a porcelain doll to each other, never done anything wrong, never thought a wrong thing, never smelled badly, never coughed or told a joke in poor taste or used the wrong fork. Oh the scrumptious first moments of virgin unfamiliarity! And to have Shakespeare as well!

We riffed more on Macbeth and then about how cold it is as Wenna got around to sloshing some (distinctly rotten) peas onto our plates. The next day at chow we showed up at the same time again and this time he smiled at me first and widely.

His name is Jorge Andersen, and yes he is a Dutchman (can I spot them or what?!) the first of his family born here. His parents emigrated with a whole church from Amsterdam and Jorge doesn't speak really southern. It's sort of southern but it's flavored with how all the people in his little Dutch community spoke growing up. They all moved to Alabama when Jorge was a lad and his family took over a dry goods store near Pelham and it was there he grew to manhood and enlisted. He knows Hawthorne in and out, and unlike most of us southerners who dissect Harriet Beecher Stowe, Jorge has actually read the thing! can quote it liberally from memory. He can do a quite respectable Marc Anthony in the funeral oration from 'Julus Ceasar'. Wonderful voice! And he sounds so European and high-toned just speaking anything at all!

For the last week we've eaten all our evening meals together, sat on the same log, looking for all the world like two world-weary men. Real men. Gruff-like and no affection. Spitting on the ground and grunting. Scratching. As a matter of fact I have no way of knowing if he feels anything for me like I already know I feel for him. I have no intentions of seeking out his sentiments. I'm just happy for someone to share my meals with, someone who will smile at me.

There are rumors we may be moving out any day now. Of course, rumors like this take life in camp and go 'round the gossip chain with the velocity of the telegraph almost weekly. Every week it's something new: we're set to move north, we're set to move south, we're going to Virginia, we're going to stay right here in

Montgomery the whole war, camped out on the capital grounds, we're going to turn into pumpkins at midnight and roll away. I'm convinced no one but Bob Lee knows what's going to happen if indeed he does. But something about the intensity of these new rumors gives me pause. Perhaps its that this is the first one Sergeant Major hasn't resolutely quashed upon hearing. That lends credence to the matter for a lot of the men. So perhaps I shall be writing you from a new campsite soon.

And I'm going to take a stand with you, sister. You say you've never seen a homsexual. What do you think Mr. Jared is, just some doughy, effiminate piano teacher who never happened to find the right girl to marry? I am hurt at your lack of support and as long as you feel it's okay to shutter your heart from me at this needy juncture, I'll just no longer indulge your TRULY IRRATIONAL views of the stepfamily and your convictions that one of them is going to sneak up someday and hit you on top of the head with a hammer. You withhold from me, I withhold from you.

Your loving brother,
Albert

My dear Albert;

Sad news Bartholomew Jr. was found two days ago, quite dead, very wet, wrapped around a barker branch in Drakes Creek twenty miles from the house. The day after he left it rain'd heavy and kept on doing so for several days. He'd apparently tried to ford a creek in deeper water than he suspected it was with a current swifter than he knew, and I know how weak he was from the consumption when he left, so he must have been really puny several days later and the Lord knows the poor stupid boy never could hunt, couldn't even gather berries or find his hind end with a stick. So, being weak and disorganized about the brain, he must've wandered into the creek, been carried off and drown'd.

The house is envelop'd in sadness this eve. The minister just left and we have Bart Jr's body in the parlor. He smells like bluegill.

Stepfather is beside himself. Darcy seems a bit broken up. Melanie seems more concerned with what to wear when the beriev'd show up to offer anyone comfort. As usual, I'm doing what cooking and what handiwork need be done with visitors coming around and a swampy body in the frontroom. We should hold services and bury him tomorrow, if it doesn't rain again, and I hope it doesn't because if Bart isn't in the ground tomorrow, he'll be harder on our nostrils in death than he ever was on our good natures in life.

Must go attend to things, hope this letter finds you well and unharmed. Life is a fragile thing. I think of you often, and pray for you nightly. I know you think I'm a bit unstable about things, easily frightened, but I do relish life, my brother, no more so than when I gaze down at Bart Jr.'s smelly head, and his father looks at me like he'd so trade me into that casket to have his beloved boy back. They hate me.

Your loving sister;
Elsie

20, NOV., 1861

11-28-61

Dearest Sister Elsie;

Exciting news! We're on the move! Not much time to write. The postmaster is coming by so I must address this quickly! We're about to board our second troop train. The first one took us to Birmingham (from whence I write you now . . .) the next train, I don't know where it's taking us—not ours to know. I don't even think Sergeant Major knows. They're awfully secretive about this stuff, spies you know. Can't have the knowledge just rampant about where thousands of armed Confederate men are bound, can you? I can understand that. SO I suppose I'll know where we're bound when I get there. Well I see the postmaster, must lick and stick,

love you.
Albert

PS
Shame about Bart!

My dear Albert;

I see how soldiering has made you hard. I see that in your attitude about Bart. I know that something in your letter to him had to have inspired him to take up arms for his country in spite of his frale condition. And you write of yrself so unmanlike!. I can see you on the glorious field of battle inspiring your fellow soldiers in a glorious way. And you question your manliness!

    Stepfather sits at the eating table unmoving day in and day out, looking down at his hands. You remember those knuckels! (How could you forget?) LOVE across one and HATE across th'other. He always said he wanted to give us more of the love hand as that was the strongest hand and then he'd laugh like it was a big joke. Never felt much like love did it, ha ha?! He's devastated about Bart. We all are well no that's not true, I'm sad but I'm not devastated. If anything happened to you I'd be devastated . . .

    The girls have an invitation to visit their Aunt Miriam in Franklin for the summer. Father thinks it would be good for them. It would be good for me I'll tell you, shaving down the number of folks I look after round the clock by two-third. I look at Stepfather and I wonder what our Mother could have ever seen in him save a chance for us to have better than otherwise we'd have had. Bart Sr. is a hard man and I am sure his lot has been hard, as is all men's in this country. This ain't New Orleans like I remember as a girl, back when Momma and Papa were still alive and I dreamt of going to school and then being a dancing girl downtown when I grew up. This is Pioneer country that man took us to and he and they are OF them and WE ain't. These are people who came where there was nothing and hack'd out lives with gumption and sweat. And these things I try to remember when he grunts at me like a dog when I bring him his coffee, or when I ask him if we should send for you, now that we're down to one man in the house and he says "Hell no!" I try to remember that he has been through much in his time, that he can be a good man, maybe. That he at least took us into his home and loved us as the Bible says to, even if he did not like us, or act nice, or treat us same as his true childr'n.

I'm sorry Albert. I just have no one in the world I can confess these things to. I have to live here with these people, and hear how they speak of me behind their doors! And I understand your hardness about Bart Jr.. I have that same hardness for the whole lot of them sometimes and I just ask Jesus for some extra love I can give them, even if they seem to never want to give any back, or feel they even should. I would like to propos a trucce that I promise to at listen to your feelings as you listen to mine because yur right we need each other's kindness and condolence even though how I feel about these people and how I know they feel about me is a WHOLE OTHER DIFFERNT affair than the fact what yu've got the notion you would like to be with a man in a way that is a perversion of the flesh and condemned by OUR LORD.

Please carry my prayers with you. You are not alone Albert. I will always be your sister and I will always love you. You've certainly not had it easy. You are a sensitive person and always were and I just wish you wouldn't worry yourself into such type homosexual hysterics. You're man enough to shoulder a gun and march forward for our fine cause of Confederates keeping this land for ourselves, out of *the hands of the Eestern Conglomerations and republican Lincolnlubbards, God Praise ye and thine!*

Now I'm as uncomfortable with slavery as everybody else who's decent enough to not own them but who listens to our pennies jingle? ha! We stand alone all together, and proud just like you and I—Devereauxs in a house full of Janschses—oh I'm of one mind tonight only! I'll not go on anymore about that. Please pardon my penmanship as I've been into the Sheerry. I do that at night after everything's clean. These people hate me! I love you and now I'm writing up the side. I'm ridiculous! Take car derre brothr! Love always, Elsie

My dear Albert;

A very Merry Christmas to my favorite soldier. Santa has sent you much to keep you warm and yummies for your belly. Hope they all make it safe and sound.

I hope I didn't burden you with my own problems too much last letter out. You have a soldier's lot to carry and you make me very proud like any sister would be.

It has now been long enough for me to be worried that I've not heard from you. I am of course praying that this package finds you healthy and you enjoy the treats with the charming Mr. Andersen on a friendly stump someplace and the safe end of a soldier's day.

I hope you enjoy the blueberry tarts and I hope the apple butter makes it without the container braking open. I know how you love to see the paper so I sent that along as well. I hope it all makes it to you without being theiv'd somewhere along the line! There's a hot place in Hell for someone who would steal food out of a package being sent to a Soldier in Arms! I hope the long woolens fit and don't itch too bad.

The house saw its first merriment since Bart was alive recently. The girls had a holiday fancy dress ball if you want to call it that out here at the house they invited friends from town and I think about half of who they invited showed up and that was enough to have the house fluttery with hankerchieves like the place had sprouted wings and you had all these girls walking around in skirts too big for the doorframes and getting stuck going in and out and it's all I could do to not bolt all the doors and set the whole place on fire.

Tommy Womack

Now Stepfather had the gall to try and sort of explain at undue length how this here fancy dress ball was more for them and their friends than for me or for any of whatever friends I might have, if I ever got a chance to make any. I asked him 'have you noticed who cleans up everything around here?' and you know how he answered me Albert? 'They clean their own rooms!' is what he thunder'd back at me! 'They clean their own rooms!' And then he stomp'd off and we hadn't spoke in two days now.

Until recently I hadn't appreciated how much I relied on having you here to talk to and keep a level head about things. I guess I held up good the first year but not lately anymore. I'm hearing their voices through the ceiling all the time now. And they sure do get me bothered. Sometimes I hear Bart Jr. talking upstairs to the girls plain as I hear the birds sing. I only hear his voice with my head down in the pillow. When I sit up, he goes away. It's terrible frightening.

The afternoon papers carry news of your units' advancing to Birmingham! So now I know you are on the move! You are in my prayers and I know that God will watch on thee o'er on the field of battle. I am ashamed of myself for going on and on about how sorry and sad I get about things around here. There is nar an hour goes by I don't face towards the south and invoke our Lord's Name in devoted prayer for you out there wherever you are.

In the spirit of the Season I want you to feel you can tell me about Mr. Andersen. I'd rather you feel like you had someone to talk to even if I don't approve or understand. God tells us to hate the sin but love the sinner. Besides, it's not in the Ten Commandments, unless it counts as adultery I suppose.

Please write when you can dear brother. God be with you and always at your side.

Love always, Marry Christmas
Elsie

18, DEC., '61

February 3rd, 1862

Dearest Elsie;

A postcard they call it! The man swears it will come
to you just like mail! Sorry haven't written. Thank you
for the Christmas presents. We marked the holidays
with DYSENTERY and it has not been a holiday I'll
want to repeat. Have receiv'd your letters, have been
marching, vomiting and voiding my bowels all over
Alabama. Will write soon.

I pray for you as well for strength to deal with all
you must.

The voices again? DON'T LISTEN TO THE
VOICES! We've been through this.

Oh! Everyone will see this! Hello everyone!

Yours ever
Albert

PS
I'm in love! And where do you get the idea any such is
condemned by OUR LORD. I'v been thru all four
Gospels of Our Saviour's life and nowhere does he teach
specifically against it. As a matter of fact haven't you read
that bit about 'the Desciple Whom Jesus Loved'. ???
Rests his head against his BREAST? It doesn't say they
met arm-wrestling or fighting over a girl does it? Ha!

Dearest Brother;

You're in love and Joy! Joy! What is her name and how did you meet her?

Cannot write long. The Yankees have occupied Clarksville and things are madness here. I am afraid to send you edibles as I don't know where you are or if they will make it to you in any presentable state, or if they will make it to you at all. The Yankees are taking anything that is not nailed down I hear that mail without packages has a better chance of going through than mail without. I also hear no mail makes it through and that Yankees are thieving and pillaging and visitng horror upon womenfolk. These awful Northerners respect nothing, not mail, not innocense, not politeness. I hope this makes it to you and that you and your new lady friend have a felicitous time, however that is managed by soldiers.

All my love,
Elsie

21, FEB, 1862

March 30th, 1862

Dearest Sister Elsie;

Greetings from Corinth, Mississippi and from the amount of marching I'v done I can't believe we're not in Indiana yet! Oh, my feet! My thighs! My knees! I say, if soldiering is all about this marching in the rain business, then I've had all the soldiering I need to last me.

We got off troop train at the point from whence there was no more rail to ride and that was a full week ago. We've been on dirt road, a long line of marching soldiers, ever since. When it's hot and dry, the dust rises up and cloaks us all. When it rains, we're the longest line of wet and miserable fellows you ever did see.

I have not seen any of what you'd call real action yet but I've heard it far off once or twice when nearby fellows routed out Union spy parties and suchlike. We just know about as much as you in Clarksville I reckon about where they are or whenever we're to meet them head on. I just remember reading in that paper way back that the Union sent Grant with a full army to the Mississippi River. And the way we're marching (and not stopping!) I reckon we've all got to run into each other sooner or later! We all know that now. It colors all conversations anymore. The roughhouse types are all a bit more serious these days. Gunfire in the distance, real stuff, not anyone practicing, it changes a man.

As we haven't been getting much mail and I have not heard from you in months I will only assume you got my postcard, and as I put in my postcard, yes, I am in love and most certainly still am now. Jorge and I have dinner every night and each occasion has given me more fuel to banish any such notions you have about homosexuals being in the same league with vampyres, trolls or Rip Van Winkle. This is not to say we've consumated a relationship in any way, nor have we even held hands, kissed or even embraced innocuously such as brothers might. None of that. But I am in love all the same, let me assure you of that, dear sister! I am in love and it is no more the imaginings of a confused young man than it is false and figmentary the beauty that comes from the piano to one's ears when played to please God. Oh, it is real sister!

After supper last night we took a walk around the area, a short one, as walking doesn't have the same relaxing effect it ordinarily does when you've already done 20 miles of it that day already under the less felicitous guise of "marching". We'd heard about some delightful springs in and amongst caves and sinkholes and giant willow trees that seem to invite the discomfited, and thus we strolled off to surfeit ourselves with such tranquility if we could find it.

Not fifteen minutes of walking brought us upon Eden itself. The willows hung like green draperies and a small pool of water presented itself with rocks at the side just large enough for a man to sit on and dive in, and no moss, no mud. It was clear all the way to the pebbles on the bottom. "Shall we have a swim?" I quip't.

I was just half-jesting but Jorge didn't need a further prod! Off came his shirt! He folded it sat it on a rock and then off came his hat and he sat that on his shirt, and then off came the trousers! He was wearing nothing underneath and I fought a gladiator's battle within myself as whether to gaze upon his beauty unceasing, or busy myself stripping down and folding my own things on my own rock, and before I knew it we were dived in, splashing naked and joyously bobbing like otters, dunking our heads, feeling cooler and cleaner than we had in a long while.

The water darkened his hair and brought it clinging to his skull. I could see further his handsomeness then because the effect made his head look larger, his jaw firmer. After a few minutes we found ourselves doing what people do when they swim. You always go a bit out in the water, stretch your arms out, lay your head back so that water flirts into your ear with loud cavey gurgles, and look at the sky, which in our case was just going purple with dusk. A glance at the vastness of our sphere while fatigued and naked brings out the philosopher in a man, I suppose.

I wanted desperately to say something like "I'm so gratfeul for your dinner company, Andersen." That's how we talk to each other. Men do that. He's Andersen to me and I'm Devereaux to him. But not wanting to "show my hand" (ironic choice of words I was showing more than my hand at the time ha!) I said "so I suppose we're going to have our big day of reckoning directly."

He reacted firercely to my innocuous attempt at conversation and I felt flushed and embarrass'd. "Do you think we shall?" he said, "and whom should we reckon to? Superior officers? We are not out of line in any way!

We're just enlisted men off-duty who can swim as we like and dine with whomever as we like."

The words came out of him with a defiant gust and I was cowed. "I was speaking of the war." I gulp'd out.

He was silent for a second and then said "Yes, yes of course! The war!"

I took his bait though, bursting as I was to speak of any of this anyway, so I added "but of course, I agree that we can dine with whomever we choose, and may I say, Andersen, I'm so delighted with your supping company. The meals have been decidedly less lonely since I've found someone to . . . eat with." We were just splashing the water back and forth, standing in the crick up to our collarbones, kicking our legs back, looking at the sky, the overhanging branches.

"It has been some lonely times in this Maaaannn's camp, yes." he mused. And that's how he said it . . . Maaaannnnn's.

"You as well?" I asked.

"Aye!" he replied. He says things like that, Aye! He calls his mother "Mutti" in the letters he writes and one day he was pining for a "mac" as we were walking in the rain, trying not to let the rain spatter our peas. He just sort of assumed I'd know that was a raincoat, but not having grown up in a Dutch religious community, I didn't.

So we swam about for a few more minutes and it began to get dark and the dreaded Mississippi skeeters showed up. We'd hoped they hadn't come out of their winter cocoons yet but a few choice bites in very sensitive places let me know they most certainly are awake and in force for the season.

We got out of the water and dressed on the rocks. I didn't know what to do. I wanted to embrace him. I wanted to kiss him. I was terrified of him decking me, of it being a giant miscalculation for me to give any demonstration towards him of affection or God forbid plain lust like I felt. There's another proof for you sister. Lust. You can't imagine a lust. You either feel lust or you don't, and watching Jorge Andersen pull up up his trousers past his dimpled hairless derrierre' inspired in me a level of appreciation for the human frame beyond any bloodless daVinci sketch-type musings on the mundane artistic beauty of the basic human frame, no this is a want to possess you cannot conjure in imaginings. It is LUST and oh it is real, sister!

We were walking back and I said "Now Andersen, we'll not carry any coals back in camp!"

"Nay, Devereaux!" he responded, "for we'll be cholers!" You recognize that? From "Romeo and Juliet" it is! On the outskirts of camp we saw Colonel Halbersted who is universally despised and we both bit our thumbs at the same time carrying on the same bit from R & J, and we both said at the same time "Yes, I DO bite my thumb, sir!" under our breaths at the same time and oh did we have a laugh over that!

Back approaching my tent-half, we parted for the evening with a handshake. Several lads in my company—Cpl. Rawlings' mob—were around, smoking, spitting, scratching. I feel them watching me everyday for some excuse to tag me the runt bunny in need of its' little balls being chewed off. With horrid impoliteness such as is only capable by the ecstatically stupid one of them hollared out ""d'ja get a kiss, Devro?" and I'm sure Jorge was still in earshot though he didn't turn around. So of course another one yelled it louder and then all Rawling's mob collapsed in fitful giggles like the funniest joke ever had just been told. I was horribly embarrased and once again horribly alone and just kept walking back to my unit as I heard them all making kissing noises with their lips. There's no sense in challenging them. What's one against ten? And they'd LOVE to pounce. You talk about the hate in that house?, try love on your own side of the fence! People will hate you then! God, if they'd caught us in that pond naked . . . . . . ?!

It is later now, I've had a bit of a private cry, best as a soldier can have in this setting, and I'm writing by the campfire light as Big Jim is playing his spoons, Walter Harding his fiddle, and both of them a bit tipsy on the Oh Be Joyful or just OBJ as it's known here. Lord knows where they got it and boy will take the hair out of your nose! They're leading whomever they can get to listen in an endless rendition of "Turkey in the Straw". I have a little tin cup of the stuff myself and it's taken the edge off the Rawling bunch's teasing, though it's rather intensified my emotions as regarding Mr. Andersen. I find myself reminiscing for him right now like he's someone I knew years ago. We had a lovely swim tonight. The loveliest time I've had in a while I do say. It is late. I must sleep. We march on the morrow, yet again!

Love,
Albert

March 31st, 1862

Dearest Elsie;

We didn't march today after all, praise God. It was actually a rather relaxing day. Most unusual that! An old crusty Sargeant, Cruller is his name, says we got the day off because we're going to need the strength and soon. I asked how he knew anything and he said "Son, I was in the Mexican campaign with Zack Taylor and before ever' battle my knee swole up like a dead fish in the sun. Now look at this knee!" so he pulled his pants leg up and sure enough it was swollen awful. We'll see if he knows what he's talking about.

Went swimming again tonight. The cat was way out of the bag about Eden, though. You can't keep a secret like that I suppose. This time there were thirty men bathing if there was one and it was all ruin't for me. None of the idyll of the night before. This time it was yahoos swinging off a rope and splashing water and acting like babies in a tub. So Jorge and I indulged a dip, then dressed and went for a stroll, a more enticing notion when you haven't marched all day, and when your new favorite swimming hole has been polluted by groundlings.

We were walking back to camp and we were asking each other how we came to enlist. I told him I'd been in a fight with my Stepfather, a rather public one downtown right in front of my piano teacher's house, and Stepfather questioned my manliness in a most vocal and public manner. Thusly, I explained, feeling the onus to prove such stature as he doubted, went straightaway to the bounty man and tried to enlist but he wouldn't take me, so I got drunk on a train to Nashville, got drunker on another to Birmingham and there I enlisted one headsplitting morning, making up a bunch of bullshine about being from Coffee County Alabama, and before I knew it I was sleeping on the State Capitol grounds in Montgomery, learning my about-face from left-right-left.

And you, I asked?

"In Pelham, I got a young lady in a family way; and it was suggested I make myself scarce for the balance of the decade." He replied matter of factly.

As you might guess, I was crushed beyond recusitation.

"Ah, I see." I think is all I said. "So you are a father now?" I asked.

"Yes." he sighed and he twirled a little branch in his hands, then made little designs with it in the dust of the road as he looked towards the red sky in the west. It was coming on nighttime.

"I'm sorry to hear that." I said.

"Oh? Why?" he asked.

I was not expecting that. It was like when a child asks why ridiculously, when the answer's obvious.

"Well, I'm just sorry to hear that." I said.

"You are sorry to hear I am not homosexual." He said.

I had no answer for that.

"You're a very handsome fellow. I think the bounty man wouldn't take you because he knew what you were about and he wanted you for himself." he then said, laughing! The nerve of the rake!

"What are you getting at?" I asked. It's amazing how a man will put up a front immediately. Me? A homosexual! What!? Well, I never!

"I think I love a lot of people." Jorge then said, gazing at the skyline. "I love too much. I loved this girl in Pelham. Stacy's her name. She's in a priory in Mobile now. Who knows where the baby's off to? The family hates me. And there was an incident with a travelling tintypist not long hence, and it was just ascribed better by everyone if I just . . . left. The war was very conveniently arranged just for me, I think. Handsome fellow, that tintypist."

My head was spinning. Jorge's hair was so gorgeously blonde from the sun. I found myself transfixed on a little gap between his front teeth, his blue eyes through Dutch slits—oh what a handsome man!

"So you have been with women and men?" I believe is what I blurted out eventually.

"Yes, Albert, I have." He was smiling all calm and I was all nervous, the silence drew out an intolerable length to me. Tho Jorge looked the picture of Peace. He wasn't uncomfortable with anything in the whole wide world at that moment. It was all me.

"Which do you prefer?" I asked then and thought stupid question, stupid stupid stupid!

He just said "I think I love people, too much maybe. I don't prefer a man over a woman any more than I prefer roast beef over smoked ham. They're both delicious and love is love, don't you think?"

We walked on a bit.

"Do you like me?" I asked.

"Oh I like you very much, Albert."

My heart soared.

"But I feel like I want to prove something. I'm here because of my Lothario ways. I want to show I can be a professional, a man, a soldier, you see. I want to kiss you right now. But the minute we kiss then Corporal Rawlings comes from behind that tree." Jorge said, pointing at a large beech nearby. I was suddenly so thrilled and relieved and more in love than ever because he was so darn right, saying everything I wanted to hear and taking the pressure out of the situation entirely.

"You know that lardass?" I assented.

"Who doesn't know that dumb ass?!" Jorge thunder'd and we both laughed out lolud and manly. "I know about fifty other Corporals just like him, and a good many like him of higher rank too!

"No Albert, I want to take you for champagne and oysters when the war is over. I want to sit with you and watch "Richard III" at the Opera House in Birmingham. After the war. Once we've proven our stature on the fields of Glory! Once we've done out part for the Grand Gay old South! No, you are a mighty handsome man Albert Devereaux and should we kiss I want it to be without fear and with absolutely no looking from side to side in the Mississippi woods. You're too handsome for any distractions from ignorants to despoil and poison such ecstacy."

And so I'm more in love than ever, but at least a bit satisfied how people get when they at least talk about something. Are you convinced now, sister?

A bit later now! There is much excitement! At almost the same time two different scouts came flying back into camp from two different paths into the northland and they both had the same tale to tell of great columns of blue suits and Stars and Stripes flags! Both scouts came across the same huge Yankee army! This may be our day of reckoning on the approach, the day when all the training and toughening we've been put through will be put to the test. One of the scouts had the army fifteen miles to the north, the other twenty milesh.

A third scout has just come in saying that Yankees may be no more than ten miles away as I write these words!

A bit later now! We attack at dawn is what I hear.

By the time you receive this the die may already be cast and fate may well have had its way with us. I know you pray for me daily and I know the Stepfamily doesn't and that is a shame. We've lived in their house without benefit of their love and Christian charity for so much of our lives now that it feels well-ordered for it to be that way, queerly.

Of course, dear Elsie, I am not the one who has to live with them now such as you do, and I am so sorry for all they put you through. You're always so much better about not hearing voices when you are calm and at peace in your world. I hope someday you find the way to drive it into their skulls that you are more than their charwoman. Some day you'll come out on top. I believe that. You must too.

Now be with me in your thoughts and prayers my

sister, as I fear it won't be long until all this training comes to a purpose and I can show the world that I am truly a man as much as any man.

And perhaps I can show that to you too.

All my love as ever,
Albert

My dear Brother;

*I humbly besech the Lord most high that this letter finds you
safe and unharmed. The papers are full of nothing now but
Shiloh and the horrendous battle. Your regiment number is
in the news accounts with much accounting of casualties but
no names and it is torture! I know you were there, we hear
so much of the agonies there, and I write this not knowing if
you are even alive to read it. I will just write to you with
feven't faith in God's grace that you are alive and will see it,
and that all is well.*

*The Yankees are sure well equip't and thankfully not too
needy. The other day a blue hatted, flag-waving patrol came
down the pike towards us. They stopped in at each house
along the way, took a few things here and there they judged
valuable to their war effort (strong wagons and any kind of
boat generally), and moved on. Mr. Hopkins gave them grief
and they spil't his sorghum over it and took his chickens.
When they called on us and found out Stepfather was a
Union veteran of the Mexican campaign, they left us pretty
much alone. For once I'm glad he's around ha! All the same
we drove the horses, cows and pigs into the woods and didn't
summon them with the bell until well after dark.*

*The Stars and Stripes flies over the Courthouse now. It
pains me to know you're fighting against a power that has
overridden your own home now.*

*The girls left just yesterday for a spring and summer with
their Aunt Miriam in Franklin. They were fighting (again)
even as the carriage left the house with their trunks full of
more stuff of life than any four whole Queens would ever
need. I told them the Yankee's will stop their carriage and*

The Lavender Boys and Elsie

take the trunks just for the trunks themselves and leave the dresses on the ground and they may visit horror upon you two girls. They told me I was a terrible person to even think such evil and that they'd be fine thank you very much. So I'll do my best to pray for the strength to remember them to Jesus with the fervence I should to be a righteous person.

If tonight's anby way of telling, the summer will consist of Stepfather sitting at the table poring over his documents with humourless quiet involvement whilst I clean the house around him, wash clothes, cook all the food, milk the cow, hay the horses, tend the garden and do all manner of things which it seems is equivalent value to my rent and nothing more—nothing worthy of love, or respect, or even a simple thanks.

This Mister Andersen sounds like a total rapscallion. You stop this swimming business with him! And you be careful how you toy with the knowings of our Lord and Saviour. Jesus was perfect and above such as flesh and sparking. And besides the Old Testament is very clear about homosexuals and about a thousand other things to keep us busy in remembrance and righteous acts throughout the day.

Your loving sister;
Elsie

12 Apr. '62

My dear sister Elsie;

I your veteran brother alive by the grace of God and
at last able to hold a pen again undertake to write to
you. I hope you are well. I am alive. I am miraculously,
unbelieveably unhurt (once the scars heal!). Surely God's
mercy is with me and I feel your blessed prayers and
thank you.

I know when you become a man now. It happens
after you've been the scaredest you can get, been to that
darkest place where fear is thick, blood is in your
temples and smoke in your eyes. You come away from
that knowing you are now a man and you don't want to
ever visit this darkest place ever again.

It will make all days hereafter worse I know, because
a man can only go into battle for the first time once. I
know that now—and I sorely cherish that ignorance I
didn't even know I had up until that moment when the
veil was rent away. The next time we are called to the
field of valor, I'll know too well what's on the way and
I do not relish that wareness.

For the first time since enlisting, I was back on my
Tennessee soil but I've never felt so far away from home
and so far off lonesomely away from everything good,
comforting, sweet or refined. My wrist is very sore from
trying to write (took a glancing blow from a musket
ball on my arm), and my head is still heavily and
comcially bandaged (an exploding shell put a great
chunk of tree in my face). Those wounds, a sore ankle
and some bruises are the extent of my injuries, pretty
good compared to many. I'm alive with all my person

and faculties. A lot of men are not—Corporal Rawlings and Sargeant Major—Jorge Andersen.

For three solid days I stood in a line as long and far as I could see through the skinny trees and overgrowth, with of all my fellow soldiers, all the fellows who've tormented me and called me vile names for a year, and we loaded our weapons and shot at Yankees while standing in that line, and then we loaded again and shot again. And again and again. Men screamed with pain next to me as their number came up. And we weren't to look. Just load and fire, again and again and again. Men on either side of me fell, and they screamed for their mothers, and cannons fired! My God, the cannons! The cannons! Have you ever heard a cannon fire, Sister? One cannon firing AWAY from you is terrifically unsettling and twenty pointed TOWARD you will leave the shit running down your legs, pardon my language.

At some point every so often our line would collapse and the field would degenerate into chaos because in the smoke you couldn't see which direction you ought to be running. Sometimes I would find myself running forward, sometimes running back and sometimes wondering which is which. I would shoot my rifle, swing a sword I found on the field and kept, and in the midst of all this amazing things happened! Three times I shot men dead in the last moment before they charged into my face, not once nor twice but three times! Three men all fell inches from me in a dire attempt to kill me, and while I worried and prayed about the prospects for their fourth I was attacked in the wrist by the musket ball. I was spinning in pain from that and headed towards the rear, gripping my howling and bleeding limb. It is then I heard a great artillery shell whistle in, landing in the branches of a tree near me. It detonated, sending great chunks of tree truck and large branches hurtling into men, obliterating some outright, sending a hefty chunk of raw lumber into my cheekbone.

Lying in the grass, feeling of my face, grateful my eyes could see and ears could still hear, I saw a young man who reviles me and calls me a Kansas City Boy and was always saying why don't yew and Andersen go suck each other?! One of those. He was crying like a damned baby, sitting on his butt and tearing at the grass with his hands, Yankees running past him without regard, the ultimate soldier's insult not to see him as a threat worth killing.

If you read in the papers of a place called "the Hornet's Nest", I was there! It was so named because the balls were flying so thick it sounded like buzzing of hornets. Jorge was there too. That was the last place I saw him and the last place you'd ever want anyone you loved to ever be. I remember his perfect face and nothing wrong with him, firing and loading with a magnificent sneer. But things were so frantic I never saw what happened, and never saw him again. He is gone. That I know. He's been tagged. I've read it. I never saw his body and never will. I was miles away for days in a hospital tent and now I'm under my tent-half even further away, and it rankles to have never seen his beautiful features in death's mask. I feel I've been robbed of some sort of completion and so he will always be a little bit alive for me inside. I will always love him.

My only friend in this whole armada of men is perished and gone to his reward, never to share his hard tack and black-eyed peas on a stump with me again. I'll never swim without thinking of him again. I know my heart will feel worse about it later. I will miss him so.

So many men in my company are either dead or so greviously injured, there is talk of folding the rest of us up into other companies and regiments. I don't know what's to happen yet. Nobody seems to know anything. Lines of command are a fuzzy. You go off to get orders from someone and then you find out that particular someone is dead, and the next in command is dead as well, so you go back to camp and sit without learning anything.

Nobody seems to even know who won or lost! All we know for sure is that while the Yankees might be disagreeable sorts with nasal voices and bad temperaments, they do fight fiercely. I'm sure they know the same of us now too, whatever they thought of us before, they know what our lead tastes like now. It's in everybody's mouth now for surely.

For months all the talk was 'wait until we get in this battle and it'll be over in a week!' Well, nobody's talking like that now. Most of the lads who talked that way will never talk again.

I remember the field hospital tent. A big fat male nurse was dressing my head wound. He smiled and said to me "I know you. You're Flamingo!"

And I said "Excuse me?"

And he said again "You're Flamingo! You were keeping company with that handsome Dutchman." and

Tommy Womack

then he moved in closer and whispered conspiratorially to me so no one else could hear "That's what we all call you, Flamingo. All us male nurses. You see that one over there?" he pointed over to a large male nurse padding fawnlike between wounded men, "He thinks you're handsome!"

So I digested this bit of information, and I can't help but admit I looked over the male nurse to see if I found him handsome as well. He looked over as if he knew we were talking about him. He smiled, we smiled back. I didn't find him attractive. A bit fat like his friend. All these nurses eat like pigs and do no marching.

"Why do you call me Flamingo?" I asked.

"Because you walk like a Flamingo, very lightly and delicately upon the ground!" he replied.

"I do not!" I thundered most indignant-like.

"Oh dear heart, you do!" he giggled back at me. I tensed up as if I were to hit him. "Well, don't be mad at me!" he implored, "God made you how he wanted you."

Then he said "you know, I could find you work among the nurses. You'd be more comfortable among us. We have teas and book group" Teas and book group!

I said thank you but I'm a soldier whether I walk like a god-damned Flamingo or not and I stomped away with my bandage flailing undone! I'll admit I'm broken hearted. I walk lightly. I'm a Flamingo, a Kansas City Boy, a Fabulous Fred.

Well I'm exhausted, my dear sister. Exhausted but alive. We start marching in the morning so I am told. I am an orphan without regiment. My whole company was evacuated to the south while I was recuperating.

I'm to join up with troops and travel with the 36th
Tennessee. Where we're bound I do not know but I
hear Chattanooga. I will write you soon.

Your loving brother,
Albert

PS,
Don't call Jorge a rapscallion again! Is it too much to ask
a sister to PRETEND to understand? You don't even
have to really understand, just MAKE LIKE! For God's
sake, woman! You're all I have in this world!

And please send good things to eat. Wenna is gone.
Six other Negroes disappeared at the same time. A little
water carrier boy said "Wenna wen' up Nawth to
'Shgago! She gwine jine up wid her hudbun! An' you kin
thank Mid Tubman's RAILroad fo dat!" So anyway,
please send good things to eat as the Corporal they put
in Wenna's stead couldn't boil water without burning it,
and we are wasting away! We chew our hard tack like it
was a delicacy anymore. The days of endless black-eyed
peas are of sudden to appear like days of feasting.
Love, A

PPS
Did I mention don't slur the good name of Jorge
Andersen anymore? I just wanted to make sure.
I am serious!

May 12th, 1862

My dear sister;

It is before reveille. I am up early and well hung-over.
You know how I am when I drink. Or perhaps you
might not. Anyway, when I drink I wake up early.
Too early. So here I am writing by taperlight as the
first rays creep over the horizon. We're moving out
today, to join the fight where we're needed back east
I understand.

To explain the drink you must understand that I have
a tentmate now (and thus a tent as well!).

And my tentmate drinks. God help me, does he drink!

Two days ago he was escorted up to me by Corporal
Natcher who hates me. "Here's a mate for you!" he said
and slung this skinny little musachioed buccanneer at me.

This fellow was not much taller than the bushes
around the tents with a little pencil moustache, huge
eyes, buck teeth like a mule's and an unruly shock of jet
black hair.

He stuck out his hands straight ahead of himkself,
walked forward and huggged the stuffing out of me.
"Flamingo!" he exclaimed happily, like we'd known each
other all our lives.

I could smell apple brandy on him.

"Oh, I've DREAMED about us being together!"
he yelped, squeezing his face to my cheek with his
hands idly brushing my buttocks in a very quick
faux-accidental manner.

Before I could even think he was off and running

with a high quality snake-oil spiel like you never heard. "You and I are going to show all these other pansies how it's DONE! We're gonna kick some Yankee ASS! We are!" He talked and bounced around in little half circles this way and then that, with one little hand out, the palm flat down, swinging back and forth like the piston on a steam engine.

So we joined our canvas halves into my first ever tent and he didn't stop talking until taps, and then he started up again as soon as taps was played.

You know me, Elsie, I'm a get-alongable, live and let live type, a listener as much as a talker, so I found myself the head-nodding yin to his loquacious yang. The hour grew late as I learned his story and drank his apple brandy with him.

His name is Private Jonathan Islip Mendlesson and he's from Savannah, Georgia. Or, as he says it "SuVANNNAH Jawdjah! Gotdammit and don't yew fuhGIT it!"

He kept pulling out a bottle of apple brandy which was almost empty, sticking it outside the tent and hollering "CHEERS, QUEERS!" then taking a great draught and handing it to me. Whenever I turned it down he'd bellow "GAAWWWWDDDDAMMIT MAYUHHN!!! We could die tommorah!"

So at some point in the late evening Private Renfro two tents down must have decided he had been cheered and queered as much as he could stand. Suddenly there he was, a big silhouette bathed in the moonlight, standing in his long underwear and glaring at Jonathan, "Mister" he said, "I am tired of your voice."

"Hush up and have a drink!" Jonathan roared and proffered the bottle of apple brandy to Renfro who knocked it out of his hand. The bottle landed and spilled out onto the grass in front of our tent. Renfro is a devout Baptist on top of other shortcomings.

Now I suppose you'd say a gauntlet had been thrown, and the last thing you'd ever expect to happen is exactly what happened. Mendelsson is quite a fey thing and see, Renfro is a big man, so it was that three days at Shiloh didn't afford me the shock and surprise I felt when Jonanthan rose from the ground like a apple brandy serpent with a lit fuse in its rear. Before you could say Jack Robinson my new tentmate had both his hands wrapped around Renfro's neck, push'd him out of the tent and they were into the grass and rolling around like growling dogs.

It was the sight to see! There must have been a hundred soldiers around the two of them inside of ten seconds, and to pandemic universal shock Renfro didn't even begin to have the better. That Jonathan Mendelsson took the surprise initiative and never let up. He is a wiry little cuss. The boys were hooting and some saying "whozzat kicking Renfro's ass?"

And somebody else I heard say "That's the rich faggot troublemaker from Georgia. His Daddy's some big To-do down 'ere."

Once my new tentmate had spent his brandyfied energy, Renfro's girth began to tip things his way. He backed up and got in a couple of good smacks that knocked Mendellson sideways. That gave Renfro just enough time to catch his breath once and then give

Mendellson one last roundhouse right to the jaw, and that's when my drunken new roomie went down like a tree.

Everyone cheered and patted Renfro on the back and led him away, just in time, as the MPs weren't far off by this time.

And wouldn't you know what happened? Up shot Mendelsson! He hopped on Renfro's back like a leapfrog! And off we were for another round! This time the MPs broke it up.

And that's how I wound up sleeping under a tent for the first time since Basic Training, and doing it alone because my new buddy was in the local jail we've commandeered as a brig, and leaving his last bottle of apple brandy around which I finished while writing this letter.

Ahh, the trumpet. Reveille. Must find coffee.

Love,
Albert

My dear brother Albert;

I thank God you are alive and in respect to the dead at least I'll speak no more about that Mr. Andersen because you are my brother and I love you and we both need each others' shoulder to lean on in these cruel and unusual times.

Much has happened here too. I must tell you because I will burst if I don't. I have been able to tell no one else and you will see why when you read.

Stepfather is dead. That's the main big news I suppose.

I'd been having serious headaches ever since the girls left and at night I would still hear their voices upstairs just like I'd been hearing Jr's and how I used to hear Momma's. I wondered at what voodoo they must know for them to be gone away and do that, because time and again I would lay my head down into the pillow and hear their voices plain as day, and then I would arise and run upstairs and would burst into their room and it would be dark and empty and motionless, then I'd go back down to my little damp bedsit by the kitchen and put my head into the pillow and I'd HEAR THEM UP THERE AGAIN. I heard them say it was my fault that I made Bart Jr. write you a letter and that you wrote him back and goaded him to join the Cause and his health failed him and so we must pay! (Did you goad him Albert? Is that true?)

So one night not long after that, Father'd been sitting at the dinner table looking over his stock certificates and documents. It was just him and me in this big house, this big old lonely house with all it's rooms and voices.

So I brought him a cup of coffee without him asking. I felt like being nice. He drank from it as if I had been asked to bring it, as if I had been expected to all along. No thanks, no looking at me, no looking anywhere but at those documents.

So then I brought him a piece of crumbcake, hot from the oven—he didn't look at it.

So then, you know the little tintype of mother that hangs on the wall? It fell.

I looked around and saw it sitting on the floor, straight up, and I could see Mother's pearl eyes looking at me from across the room.

For this, Stepfather actually turned and looked around. "Attend to that, will you." he said. Then he turned back to his documents.

So I did. I went to the barn and got the clawhammer and came back in and pull'd the nail out of the wall a bit so I could rehang the pictur and so then I was afforded a look over Father's shoulder and I read ". . . hereby bequeath all my worldly possessions to my two dearly natural born daughters, Melanie and Darcy, to be split among the two of them as they see . . ." and that's as far as I could see.

Now I know what you're thinking, your poor sister's voices in her head and all that. But then I heard Mother singing Blessed Assurance CLEAR AS DAY, and there was another voice with hers. It was Father's. Our real Father's voice. And my head WASN'T down in the pillow! I hadn't heard it in twenty years and suddenly there he was BIG AS LIFE. My skin tingled, my heart swole up in my chest and I had all the joy of being born again. You want to go on about how your manlust is real; well this voice of Father was REAL! I'm not crazy or balmy or tired or anything like that, I was just being served a genuine Bible MIRACLE.

From there it didn't take much agaonizing really. I just

did it. I've honestly fretted more about whether to have greens or beans with ham hocks. I took a step closer behind Stepfather, rose the clawhammer over my head and brought it crashing down onto his bald spotty skull! Next I knew I was raising the claw back up and pulling away bits of our Stepfather's head with it. I saw a trickle of red and white stuff flinging off to the ceiling as I pulled my arm back.

He didn't move, he didn't tremble. He didn't even bow forward. For a second it was as if he was still just looking at all the documents in front of him, except now there was a trail of red blotchy splatter going across the paper, across the table, up the far wall, up on the ceiling.

So I hit him again. And again! And then again!

After I got tired of that I stopped and sat down on the butter churn a few steps away, breathing hard, regarding my whole deed. For a second all was stillness and the whole world wasn't breathing. Then he swayed backwards and crashed to the floor right in front of me. His bleeding head was at my feet and his eyes were wide open, utterly surpris'd, looking up right at me.

Mother and Father began singing Blessed Assurance together again. It was wonderful! "Blessed Assurance, Jesus is Mine! O' what a foretaste of glory divine!"

I sat there on the churn and sang along and looked at Stepfather, a little bit of his skull flapped back and his blackberry-type blood just crep't and crep't across that old wood floor. Although a bit winded, I was as relaxed as if stretched out by a sunny brook on a gorgeous spring day. I was absolutely compos'd. Five minutes before, I'd had been searching for the claw hammer in the barn and my heart had been tense in my chest, and now these short few moments later, I'd done murder, there was a dead body at my feet and I was as peaceablly reclined as one can get with a hind end my size on top a butter churn, and our two true and dear departed parents were singing *Blessed Assurance* in beautiful harmony with me PLAIN AS DAY with my head OUT OF THE PILLOW. I joined in. I could hear my voice blending rapturously with theirs.

Such a joyous occasion! "I love you mother!" I cried, "I love you Father!" and they answered "we love you, blessed daughter."

As you might imagine I was rather busy the rest of the day. Mother and father were fantastically helpful with all the little things you have to do after you do murder. (The actual killing is the merest beginning of the chore, I've discovered now.)

"First you've got to do a bit of bloodletting." Mother quipp't.

I told her I didn't know the first thing about bloodletting and she said to drag Stepfather's carcass onto the backporch, which, with a lot of heaving and grunting, I did.

"Hang his head over the edge." she instructed. I did.

"His neck as well." Father said.

It was so nice, Albert. Having both parents together again. It was like a family outing when I was ten moreso than any mere dismembering of a dead body.

"No dear," Father intoned, "you'll want to get a good knife and make some fairly deep cuts into both sides of his neck." So I did just that. "Now go get some rope and throw it over that rafter."he said. So I did that. "Now tie the other end to his feet." he said. So I did that too. O'to hear his voice after all this time! He hasn't changed. He sounded just like he always did.

"Okay," both our parents said in unison, "Heave!" I tugg'd on the the rope and Stepfather's body rose into the air almost until his shoulder's came off the ground. Oops! Stepfather

Tommy Womack

swung off the ground, swung out a little, swung back and knocked me over! Silly me. Next time I got him hanging right.

The bloodletting got done and a large puddle of red soaked into the ground beneath the porch, then I let Stepfather clump to the porch floor again. I heard Mother and Father discussing things about how . . . "well, she can't bury him. He just has to disappear."

And then Father said "There's enough sausage on that man to feed a church all Sunday afternoon and well on to Wednesday!"

There's much else to tell you, dear brother, but I am quite tired. It is well past midnight as I write this and the last candle is about done with itself. I've had a long evening scattering ground-up bits of Stepfather all around the corn patch and finding things to do with bones and clothes, not to mention all the cleaning of the kitchen I had to do (there's still much cleaning to be done to the ceiling), and of course there's all the makings of a lovely summer sausage curing out in the smokehouse right now.

I love you always, dear brother. Mother and Father, of course, send their love. I am clasping her tintype to my breast as I write this and will take it to bed with me. If I'd have known killing Stepfather would bring us all this much closer together again, I'd've done it a long time ago.

I will pray you Godspeed in battle, blessings, Glory and deliverance from your perversions.

Much love,
Elsie

8, JUNE, '62

June 20th, 1862

My dear sister;

My, now that last letter did pack a wallop! I never knew
you had such talent! (Your grammar has come so far!
Are you studying from a primer?) I was in the mood for
some escapist fiction to be sure and you must've known,
I hope you feel better. Very realistic. You should write
for Harper's. In all seriousness! You have talent! I am
impressed. That was quite a hair-raising sketch. You
should show that to Stepfather sometime and put some
fear into him! Maybe he'll treat you better! Ha!

We've had a very hard couple of weeks, walking
across Mississippi, Alabama and now into the Carolinas.
I doubt even Wenna could make much of our meager
rations lately. The lads are starving and the other night
several fellows stole a pig and ate it raw. There's a
definite different feeling about things now since our
recent experiences. No face I see is untouched by it.

I miss Jorge powerfully. For him this is all over. Did I
tell you he wished to be a professor someday? Ah, but
he would have been handsome in tweed!

I like Jonathan more and more, though it takes most
of one's own energy being around him. He's from a fine,
fine family in Savannah, which is why he's been in and
out of the stockade the entire war with nothing more
than progressive slaps on the wrist so far. His father was
a big wheel in the Mexican Campaign. He sent
Jonathan off to Military Academy This and Military
Academy That for all his youth. Jonathan speaks very
fondly of a highly prized Lieutenant in the 104th

Tommy Womack

Alabama who's a recent top graduate of some institution Jonathan's been thrown out of.

He says he stands to inherit his father's plantation only if all his other brothers die. I asked him how many brothers he has and he took a big drink of apple brandy and said "I have two brothers and one's dead so far. Odds are even, Jack!" and he laughed really loud, like he does a lot.

He bandies the word "homosexual" like it's a political party affiliation. He say's it's Latin and not knowing any Latin I can't dispute him I don't reckon. He sure knows his books and poetry and he does love a drink. His family's all but disowned him but since he's from so high up in Savannah society there's a lot of pride involved and I figure once you're born to such circles you stay there. He speaks fondly of his grandmother, loves music, loves macrame' and is a mad flirt. I met a boy just like him once when the community choir went to Nashville once. He'd love to kiss me just to get caught and if I fell for him in any way he'd just notch me on his belt, so I know to hold my heart in check a bit around Jonathan's type.

He was let out of the stockade so he could march in formation with the rest of us (albeit handcuff'd) and you should see how he glares at everyone except me. He loves a fight. And he's strong. He looks like a wee thing but he's hard as stone and wiry as a jackass. "I like you, Flamingo," he says, "the rest of these laggards can kiss my ass, but I like you."

But on to other things . . .

All this talk of it being a short and sweet war has gone out the window. Lads are buckling down for a long haul now, doing morbid things like writing their names and hometowns on handkerchiefs or bits of paper and sewing such into the backs of their shirts so others will know who they are should they fall. I've done it. It makes you stop and think about yourself and who you are and what anybody might feel about you should you become just something to be found on the ground. 'Here lies Albert Devereaux—Send him back so his sister'll know—He died for the virtues of Valley Forge—And gave his heart to a man named Jorge.'

We are supposed to hook up with the Army of Northern Virginia is what I hear, and push north. Jonathan relishes this campaign. He wants us to march on Washington because he was a Page in Washington on the Congressional floor for a whole year as a fourteen-year-old, and he speaks fondly of several men in the Buchannan administration, says we'll have a dandy time in that town. It'll be blowjobs and oysters!, he says. (A blowjob is Government work, I've gathered.) Jonathan says it's nice work if you can get it and laughs again. Everything's a laugh to him.

He's none too retiring and being as I frankly know why they paired us, and I frankly don't wish to take anyone elses side over Jonathan's in anything, I guess I have become less retiring too. The other day one of the Sargeants called me a damn faggot and I turned around and showed him the bandage still wrap't round my head and said "is this the wound of a faggot to you, Sargeant!? I think not and I'll fight any man who says it's the wound of a faggot!" He didn't goad me any further but I felt both good and bad about it later. Good because I stood up for myself, bad because it's generally a very bad idea to talk to a Sargeant that way, and worse because I denied who I was. My face, however wounded it is, IS the face of a faggot. I don't like the word, but if I be that then I be that and may God's mercy rain down on all.

We were marching along the other day and our new Sargeant—Carver is his name—sidled up to Jonathan and me. He hissed at us "I know what yew two perverts dew in yawl's tent and a bunch of dicksuckers like yew don't have no place in this army and I intend to dew somethin' about just that!" Now, sister, I apologize for the coarseness but this weighs heavy on my brow and this thing about "dicksuckers" . . . It causes much mystery in me. Really, how crude?! I've never sucked anyone's dick. I've never sucked anyone's ANYTHING. I've never WANTED to. I don't suck anything of Jonathan's and he neither mine! He's a friend, my tentmate. I'm not looking for a romance. If I could dress in black and walk the hills for Jorge, I would. What is it with this dicksucking business? Of all images to linger over and ascribe others with!

Am much tired. I'm sorry to burden you with such harshness as is a man's life in a man's world.

Again, frightening, wonderful story! Show it to Stepfather and maybe he'll realize how crazy you COULD BE! Ha! Ha!

Much love,
Albert

PS,
I suffer no perversions.

June 24th, 1862

Dearest Sister Elsie

Two days since I last wrote and I have to write again.

You won't believe this! We were summoned to Colonel Montgomery's tent, Jonathan and I. We showed up directly and his aide, Cpl. Bailey, usher'd us into the Colonel's presence. Now if I'm any kind of Flamingo, Bailey doesn't touch the ground! I'm a gorilla dragging its knuckles across the earth next to him!

Bailey and Jonathan exchanged some sort of knowing look that they don't think I noticed but I couldn't have helped to. They smiled at each other, for Pete's sake! In this man's army, you never smile if it's official business and they exchanged big cheshire grins, they did!

So Colonel Montgomery was curt with us but with a smile in his demeanor too. He said "I understand that there may be a difference of opinions amongst your troopmates about . . . things." And then he just looked at us for the longest time. We were soon to discover that the Colonel does that, just stares at you, like the two of you share a secret and he's reflecting on it.

Jonathan started talking straightaway. I tensed up waiting for him to say something foolish but he actually came off quite erudite. "Well sir," he said, "I'll be the first to admit that my fine family's traditions and standing may have affected my mouth here and there, and my personality tends to draw me into situations that I might could otherwise should bypass. But I must say neither I nor my esteemed tentmate Private Devereaux

Tommy Womack

have ever sought to disturb matters in this camp or do anything that might cause problems in the troops or an overall breakdown in our Glroious war effort . . ." and on and on . . .

"Private Mendelsson," interrupted Colonel Montgomery, "I understand you went to the brig his first night in the regiment?" and then Jonathan knew to shut up.

Then Colonel Montgomery stood up and said "Lads, the particulars of your tent life—such as it affects nothing beyond the flaps—I neither know nor seek to know. I ask you two things while you're under my command in serviced to our Glorious Cause— shoot straight and keep your noses clean, and if I see you in here again it'll be. . . ." and he seemed to search for something to say and then he just sort of lamely added "worse than this."

Then he dismissed us. And that was it.

I must post this before the train leaves. We are off marching into dense wood and the Lord only knows when I'd have oppurtunity to mail next. Please entertain me with another sketch! Kill Darcy this time. Ha!

Much love,
Albert

PS
I still suffer no perversions.

My dear Doubting Albert;

It appears that you took my "sketch" with a bit more salt than you might ought to.

Enclosed please find the last five weeks' Harpers. Pay careful attention to the one with the blue ribbon around it. June 12th. Do not unwrap it around witnesses. Enclosed within do please discover a final token of Stepfather's "love" for you. The letter V to be exact, as it was the most recognizable still. The pickle smell comes from it having been kept in the jar with such.

I hope you are well. I'll speak no more of perversions if it will make you happy.

It is very hot around here. Too hot for much work in the fields and without more rain I fear for the corn crop.

All my love to you ever (and Mother's and Father's as well!!!)

I am most concerned with the coarse dialect you have incorporated into your correspondence. I fear for the quality of folk you've taken up with.

Much love,
Elsie

1, JULY, '62

PS
Please don't tell anyone I ever told you this, but a b--- j-- IS when you s--- a d---! It's no kind of government work you need, boy! You mustn't write things like that to your sister anymore. I am a lady, sister or no.

Tommy Womack

FROM PVT. ALBERT DEVEREAUX CONFEDERATE
ARMED FORCES DISPATCH, ASHEVILLE,
NORTH CAROLINA TO MARY ELSIE DEVEREAUX
C/O PARKER DRY GOODS CLARKSVILLE TENN
14:55 PM, 7, JULY, 1862. DEAREST
SISTER STOP HAVE RECIEVD PKG STOP AM
SPENDING LAST PENNY ON T-GRM STOP HAVE
APPLIED FOR FURLOUGH STOP IN MEANTIME
PLEASE STOP STOP PLEASE STOP STOP MUCH
LOVE ALBERT STOP

My dear brother Albert;

My first telegram! When they told me of it at Parker's I first off trembl'd and feared of the worst! But still how thoughtful of you.

I understand your concern, dear brother, but there's really no need for a furlough unless you just feel like coming home anyway, and of course if our Glorious Cause and country can spare you for the time. I would of course LOVE to see you in any circumstance the peas are coming in and it's all I can do to harvest them all (I'm a bit shorthanded now ha!) Hulling is how I pass the evenings now, which are so peaceful.

The weather is better, we've had a break from the muggies so the corn isn't looking so wilted and wan. The air has been so clear at nights that I can even see the rolling hills over the ridge and the smoke curling of the Farlis's smokehouse. At night the fireflies light up the whole valley.

I've been looking over the sows and trying to decide who to butcher. I have a feeling this year's sausage will be a prizewinner. (It'll certainly be unusual ha!)

I do hope the war effort doesn't cut too much into the fair season, because we do have such a good-looking garden this year, not to mention the stock. I hear Yankees to the west of us have plunder'd whole family's storehouses and I of course pray we don't face such.

Mother and Father's daily encouragement has been such a blessing. I carry her tintype in the pocket of my smock always and she and Father sing to me as we hoe and do chores. When I join in it's such a splendid harmony, to hear my voice blend with theirs, ringing across the open fields in front of the house I suspect I'll have enough berries in to work on a

Tommy Womack

jam cake for you this week and I hope it makes it to you on the field of battle.

Oh, how I worry and pray for you so, dear Albert. I hope you and your Jonathan are still getting along well and that he is not leading you too much into trouble and wild ways. I understand how soldiers will take a drink and I don't want to be a fuddy-duddy, but do keep free of card-playing, brother and read your Bible, as it will be a blessing and bring you strength in dealing with these feelings that pull on your heart and lead you away from a relationship with righteousness to it.

Mr. Jared says hello and wants to hear that you haven't forgotten about your piano playing. He said he longs to hear you sing in church again soon, as of course I do as well. I told him it's doubtful you get much oppurtunity to play piano as you're marching in a field with a great army, and, while you fellows haul around quite a lot of stuff I told him I relly doubted a piano was amongst it all. Still, he sends regards and hopes that when you pass a church with a piano in it that you might play some and that it would be good for your spirit to do so. You call him a homosexual? He seems a fine man to me.

Do tell me how your days are. I yearn to hear.

All my love,
Elsie

8th, JULY, '62

August 1st, 1862

My dear sister;

I am at wit's end. I've walked all the way around the camp three times with your letter in my hand. While I don't believe anyone's ever been through my letters before, I feel the need now to keep this one close to my breast though even then I fear it may burn a hole in my heart!

While I'm of course happy for whatever makes you happy, there are limits to empathy put by circumstances: such as other peoples' welfares and of course the Commandments of Almighty God.

Given the pickly-green digit that arrived in the previous mailing, and barring any further evidence that this is all some sort of cantilevered japery, I must now take your parlor sketch at face value and let the facts soak into my brian like dye into cloth. You have truly brained our Stepfather to lifelessness and dismembered his mortal remains!

In case you haven't already guess'd I have been denied a furlough 'long with all others who'd like one. We are dug in at Fredricksburg, Virginia and are expecting a prolonged and stern visitation from Billy Yank any time now. There are hardship discharges to be had of course, but I don't feel like going to Col. Montgomery and asking for a pass back to Tennessee inasmuch as my sister has taken back up with hearing voices, has done kil't and might kill again. This might more complicate than rectify matters, I fear.

Tommy Womack

If it is your experience that the tintype of Mother speaks to you, I face the inescapability that you've gone full balmy. I thusly wish I could be there to mop your brow and brew herb tea while you sleep under several blankets and sweat your fever clean, but I cannot be.

However, if this is some elaborate ruse in case our correspondence is discovered and you are haul'd in front of a judge and you should then wish to plead insanity, may I assure you that the insane asylum is no finer a home than jail. Jonathan is an alumnus of an insane asylum as his parents sent him to one in a grand attempt to mend him of his homosexualness. If anything the trip confirmed and accentuated such. He speaks with longing about a guard named Raymond.

I am too stunn'd and upset to write more now. Please do no more of this madness.

Love,
Albert

August 4th, 1862

Dearest Elsie;

Just wrote, must write again! Have had the most tremendous skirmish! Not as exciting as Shiloh but thank God for that! We walloped them this time, Elsie!

All the same I thought for a second my number was up and Gabriel wanted me for His trumpet squad. I took a blow to the right shoulder which knocked me backwards and bruised me up goodly with a big welt and some bleeding . . . And that's all!

They call it a "weak powder charge" and it happens sometimes. Generally it means the powder was wet. The ball blasts out the other fellow's barrel without as much gumption as might be needed to rend a man's flesh like is wanted. This ball slammed into me and stopped at the first layer of muscle. I'm sore as a saddle butt and swole up the size of a pig's bladder on my shoulder, but I'll be okay. Men take it as an omen, that you're being saved for a greater good.

"Oh it's Flamingo!" he hollared as I got brought into the hospital tent. It was the same male nurse as last time.

"Don't call me that!" I snapped.

"Oh sit down and let me attend to that." he said pointing at my shoulder. "You're quite talked-about, you know."

I asked why I'd ever be talked about and he explained that everybody saw me take that bullet and keep running forward, and that the whole army was impressed and everyone was talking about me. He said it's all over camp that I seized the flag after the bearer fell and rushed a Yankee position. The vaguaries of war, the excitement of the moment, I don't remember any flag at all, but he says everybody says I did it.

What's your name? I asked.

"Swindon." he said as he dressed my wound.

"Is that your first or last name?" I asked.

"Say the magic word and I'll tell." he said. I mustn't have said it, as I still don't know but I'm sorry I disapprove. My dear sister I venture that intemperate flirtatiousness ITSELF is a mightier PERVERSION of our flesh and civilized existence than is that love which dare not speak it's own name. And while it may not speak of itself openly, I have the feeling it wormed it's way into a speech full of otherwise the usual battle invective and furious scripture we get from Commanders. Colonel Montgomery gave the most amazing speech to the assembled troops the other day. I can't help but think I was part of it..

"Gentlemen," he said, amongst other stuff, as to the best of my recollection " we are gathered together these many many miles from our homes, so far from our wives and families, the people in the valleys and towns and farms where we grew up, and we are here united in a Glorious Cause, to preserve our right to be who we are, southern men! (Much cheering) There has been hewing and hahhing in the ab'litionist Yankee press about the Mo ra-li-tehhh of this war! The morality?! (Roars of indignation from all) The morality of our Glorious Cause?! We are not immoral men. I defy a single man to question a single other man's moral stature!" (you should hear him say it, sister . . . maahhhrrrl statchyahhh!!! Great cheers.) "We are MANY DIFFERENT TYPES of men, but ALL SOUTH'UN MEN!! (Profound and generous cheers all around!) Gentlemen, I hear it is said that a proper Southern man can whip a dozen Yankees. I stand before you here today to say that I KNOW that to be true!" (Much cheering. He cut it off with a sweep of his hand.)"I KNOW it to be true because it MUST be true!" he thundered and his voice rang back off a blue ridge in the distance. "For every one of those men must do his job—and do it to its fullest—for our cause to prevail." He put his hands behind his back and started to walk back and forth a little bit, "Men, there isn't a cannon foundry in the American South, not a one. We have no enforceable treaties of armament. We have one another and that is all! That is really all a people ever have, those amongst them, their friends, their tentmates, their foreign vis'tors, we need 'em all right now. Now is not a time for dividing. Now is a time for Confederate UNITY. We need every man to our cause and I ask you all . . . each and every soldier . . . to embrace his fellow man, for what he is, as he embraces you." He looked for a moment like he wished he'd chosen a word other than embrace, but he couldn't take it back now and besides that he had them, they were cheering and then he just went balmy on us. That look came across his face, that placid preacher look our Col. gets, and he kept talking then when it might have done him well to just quit right then "What I'm saying men is . . . some of us like rhubarb! As a matter of fact some of us can't stand the

Tommy Womack

smell of it. But I know MANY MANY SOLDIERS as well who are fond of rhubarb. Not many . . . no more than a few really. But a few nonetheless." (Cheers long faded, sidelong glances beginning to dart around. You can feel them in formation.) "But I implore you all, brothers in arms, Soldiers in our Glorious Cause. EMBRACE the rhubarb-lover in the tent next to you. Because I tell you no one will be eating or serving rhubarb when we stride onto the field of glory! Rhubarb is a personal matter and NOT A MILITARY CONCERN!" And he hammered that point home looking at us all so earnestly like he'd just proven the existence of God and I swear the rhubarb business has been the topic of every campfire discussion since as we haven't eaten any nor has anyone particyularly griped about not having eaten any or needing any or even talking about it. NO ONE understands this man now! I confess a certain befuddlement myself regarding metaphor but I think I appreciate the intent all the same.

He went on from there . . ."And when we all hit the field of glory, we hit it as a resolute body of the South. Gentlemen, we ARE the Confederacy! And life is to be lived like the joyous soldier's life, I say eat drink and be merry! I say if it happens not on the drill field . . . DON'T ASK!" (scattered clapping) "and those of you who insist on being outside the fence of society, (and I swear he glared right at Jonanthan for a splintered second!) DON'T TELL!!!!"

Big cheers this time, everyone heard what they wanted to hear. Most of the platoon thought he was referring to the dice games that go on constantly. I see a political future for Colonel Montgomery if he makes out of all this, pray we all do.

Later I passed a tent with a bunch of privates gabbing in front of it. I heard "whut the hell was he talking about?" "Waaalll. . . ." another one answered, "I reckon the Colonel likes rhubarb." And another one said "sumbuddy tol' me the Colonel likes to speak in metal fur." And another one said "metal fur? What the hell's that?" "Damned if I know." the previous man replied. "He warn't wearin' no fur I saw." "Shuttuup he's tawlkin' about the gamblin' and the whooores!"

So the big news doesn't stop there.

Two days ago seven fellows showed up at our tent, the nurse fellow, Swindon, and six other lads I either recognized as nurses or didn't know at all.

"We've responded to a Call to Arms for our Glorious Cause." Swindon chirped.

Jonathan he looked at me instead of talking, which led me to feel like this was a bit of a set-up, like these lads knew Jonathan better than me. That wouldn't be a surprise as Jonathan knows everyone. So Swindon said again "we've responded to a call to arms." Jonathan just kept looking at me.?! Have you ever gotten the feeling you were being put in charge of something whether you wanted it or not, sister? This was that.

Well as I'm sure you'd heard at home, there is considerable talk amongst the troops about the math involved in this match and like what Col. Montgomery was talking about with the cannon foundries and such. Well these nurse fellows are of course not unpatriotic and so full well they wish'd to serve our Glorious Cause. In the wake of a few divisions that got routed, we've been forming new regiments and taking on recruits the last month or so and that's why those fellows were here. They wanted to form a new regiment, and they wanted to form it with me as their Sargent! Can you believe that? They said they hadn't said anything to the Nurses' board or to anybody of rank yet and if I said no, then they would just go back to the hospital and get back to rolling bandages like nothing ever happened. They said I was well-respected for taking that weak powder bullet and keeping on my feet and that I would be a good Sargent, they thought.

Then Jonathan said "I think so too, besides I'll never get a stripe and you're the only other man in this Army I could stand to see a new one on!"

Well, the Oh Be Joyful flowed. And then Jonathan pulled out some hemp he'd gotten sent in the mail. He put it in a pipe and we passed it around and have you ever smoked any of that, sister? My God in Heaven! Two hours later these guys were all the best friends I'd ever had and I felt like I'd known them all my life. It was most jocular and I found their company quite comforting. I'm pleased to say over the coming days our comaraderie thickened and friendships acreted.

I was among a group of men all like me; I was not ODD! Do you know how odd it feels to finally not feel odd? So I began to seriously consider these mens' proposal. We'd obviously be a small regiment, but I think I'm going to speak to the Colonel about it. Think of it. Sargent Albert Devereaux!

I don't at all want to be coming off as casual or unconcerned about this killing business of yours . . . do you think your two stepsisters are not going to notice something amiss when they come back from Auntie Miriam's and StepFather is NOT THERE? Do you have a story? Have you thought any about what you intend to do?

When I think of this all my hand freezes around the pen. My sister the murderer. And of the quandry this puts ME in? (If two people can make a quandry.) I'd never in my life condemn you to the gallows, nor the cells. Did I love our Stepfather? No. Did he love me? No. But this doesn't get in the way of morality, nor your mental state for which I worry so.

My dear I have seen so much death and suffering in this fight so far. I'd be happy to go home and be done with it tomorrow, but as it is we're dug in and there's cannon fire to the north as I write this. And they're not letting hardly anyone go home, not hardly for sickness nor wilting farms and I doubt very much for murdering sisters hearing dead relatives talk from a tintype. So until this fight breaks, keep yourself together my love.

Your brother,
Albert

PS
When it's convenient please illuminate me as to why Mr. Jared cannot be both a homosexual AND a completely fine man?! And I think this whole war is over a few of those antique Old Testament principles

Tommy Womack

anyhow—such as the whole notion of slavery, so why stop there Sister?, let's throw more edicts on the pile, or would you prefer an adherence to the letter of the law and a man's required travel to the village outskirts for ritual cleansing after every nocturnal emission? The men in this camp would be up and down all night long were that the case.

My Dear Brother;

*Your language has gotten quite corse and plese don't call me
balmy Mother and Father say you should apologize. They say
I did us both a great favor in killing Stepfather and you are
being most unappreciative they say yur denying their
miraculess renewed place in my life must mean you also deny
all miracles—EVERY BIT of Duteronimy, and that Daniel
was not rescued in the lion's den, that Isaiah never called fire
from the sky, and that Our Saviour did not rise from his
tomb. I shuddn't be surprised at yur langage on how yu're
consorting with known Hellbound scoundrels. I pray for you
nightly and dayly, my dear Brother.*

*I am so glad to know you are still with us. The papers are
again full of horrendous details of battles and horrors but
they say good things about how our boys have done, and I'm
proud to hear how well you've done.*

*I'm sorry I can't send you much in the way of treats and
desserts. The Yankees came thru again in force, trampled the
garden and picked the smokehouse about half-gone and now
I'll never know if I spiced your Stepfather right because they
run off with the best of him and the rest went bad and I
threw it out. I really wanted to know how that blend set on
the stomach and now I won't know. I've been
experrimenting ha! What they left with was about half-
pork/half Stepfather with a lot of sage—all I had, and if you
can find anymore sage in Tennessee, please tell me where!
The War and it's shortages!*

*Might as well just come out and say it. I know it won't
thrill you, but I kill'd Darcy yesterday.*

Yep. She'd come home alone ahead of Melanie because

they were having some spat like usual. Darcy spent what must have been her last cash on a carriage and a horse and drove her own self all the way back to Clarksville! Gutsy wench!

Well, I herd a horse and cariage clip-clop down the road and was amazed because here she come up alone, no driver, no companion or anything. It was a miracle the Yankees hadn't vist'd horror upon her, maybe they did. I don't suppose we'll ever know now.

Since we'd been thru it all once already it just went like a clock, I mean, just a wonderful flow to it all. I came out onto the porch just as Darcy pulled up to a stop, she stepped out of the carriage, looked up at me and didn't even smile after two months gone! Didn't even smile! She just left all her baggage in the carriage, lifted up at her skirt with both hands and stepped out to the front step of the porch, extending her right gloved hand royally for me to help her ascend the steps like the Princess she is.

Boy! Did her eyes go wide when I brought that clawhammer down on the top of that pretty blu ribon'd skull! She just stood there for a second looking at me surprised with her mouth all trying to form some words and such as the hammer just hung there in her head, and then she went down like a sack of laundry slid all the way down the front porch backward and head- first!

Oh, the three of us had the most delightfu eveningl! Mother and Father sang hymns and I had Darcy all skinned and boned and the choice cuts hung up in the smokehouse and all the bones ground up into meal by sunup! All traces gone! They say the first murder is the hardest I believe it This one went smuth.

Well, I must run because there's still much to be done. That girl carried more luggage than anyone I ever did see.

Mother and Father send ther love and perhapps next package I can send you some pickled ladyfingers ha!

All my love,
Elsie

29, AUG., '62

September 12th, 1862

My Dear Sister Elsie;

It troubles my heart greatly to hear your most recent complications to an already wretched circumstance. It is unwelcome and heartrending news that you have kill'd again as you will now be a double murderer in the eyes of the court, an unsettlingly jolly one at that and surely to hang. "They" say the first murder is the hardest? Who is THEY? I must know who else you're sharing these adventures with besides me. I am further troubled you label my heart's desires a perversion whilst at the same time you sing hymns, bludgeon our steprelations and ruffle indignantly when I might quite rightly question your sanity over the whole thing. No dear, I do not question the miracles of the Bible. Our Saviour was Our Saviour, He can rise from the grave. Our Mother, lovely as she was, is another matter.

As to things here, we are moving north and digging in for the winter, and we're directly under Bobby Lee now. I've seen him ride by in camp. A majestic man! And I'm a good deal closer to him in rank now than I was before! Read on for details!

I presented myself at Col. Montgomery's tent one afternoon not long after the nurses had approached me and we'd had that wonderful evening with the Oh Be Joyful and the hemp and all, and I announced to Corporal Bailey I'd been approached by volunteers to Our Glorious Confederate Cause to form a new regiment and then I stopped myself before I got myself into too much of an explanation.

So Cpl. Bailey (eyes like Jorge's!) told me he'd let Col. Montgomery know I came by, and he must have in short order because I hadn't hardly gotten back to my own tent when a messenger ran up on horseback with a note in his hand and he was hollering "Devereax!" over and over. "I'm Devereaux." I said, so then he thrust the note into my hand, spun around on the horse and was off. The note said.

> COLONEL MONTGOMERY
> REQUESTS THE PLEASURE OF
> YOUR COMPANY
> FOR LATE SUPPER.
> 2100 HOURS.
> THE COLONEL'S. TENT.
> ATTIRE CASUAL.

So I didn't know what to think. Dinner with the Colonel? Me?

I showed up spot on time and the Colonel was there to greet me. He's about 45 I'd say. Lovely clean-shaven face and ringlet curls in his hair. I kept expecting others to show up, junior officers, anybody, and noone else was showing up. I kept looking at the tent door expecting such. The Colonel served me a (fine) brandy as we sat across his table with the oil lamp casting a senia glow across the expansive tent, and as I drank it and we indulged in light banter, I began to realize it was just going to be the two of us. And that's how the steward served the dinner. He brought in two plates and two covered dishes and so there I was dining with my Colonel alone. My dear, I have not eaten so well since last I was home eating your cooking! Roast beef! Oysters! Okra! Iced cherries! Oh it was a spread!

I found the Colonel to be a very charming man. He used to be in Politics before the war, some sort of adjudant of someone somehow in the Pierce and Buchannan administrations, and when Lincoln came along he seceded with his own state of South Carolina. As we ate, he spun several convivial yarns about Washington balls and how darling a man Buchannan especially is.

As the steward cleared the dishes, he served me another brandy and turned the conversation to military matters. He told me how brave he thought I'd performed at Shiloh, and then how that recent weak powder bullet was Providence's way of saving me for something greater. He said he'd heard I inspired recruits and that he thought I was officer material from the way I walked alone. (Officer material from the way I walked alone! Take that, Swindon! Score one for all flamingoes everywhere!)

"Deveraux," he said, "you're the second person since word went out who's approached me in any seriousness about new comp'ny musterings. And that first fellow's an idiot." He let that hang for a second, just looking at me, like he does.

"Tell me," he continued, "how many men have approached you? Do you feel you have, say a hundred men?" Then I relaxed because the game was up. Any notion of us being our own company were dashed on the rocks if he had any such expectations as a hundred anything!

"Actually , sir," I sighed, "counting me, Sir, we're up to . . . nine men, Sir."

He didn't seem concerned at all with that! Not at all! He just kept staring at me with that congenial gaze of his. I was beginning to think it was that look like Reverend Baker back home always has, always just sort of grinning like a benign large floppy animal.

"What men are these?" he asked me.

"Male nurses, sir." I replied.

"Swindon?" he asked immediately.

"Why yes sir, Swindon's one of them."

"Wonderful! Good man, Swindon is! Wraps a lovely bandange, Swindon does!"

The Colonel slapped his hands together, stood up and faced down at me sternly, "Sargent, armies grow like a mustard seed by the caliber of men therein who show themselves . . . To know themselves . . . in their hearts . . . you know . . . Men who know who they are!" He looked at me like I knew what he was talking about and and I didn't, I had my guesses but they seemed outlandish. He drift'd off in reverie for a second. I began to think he'd had his limit of brandy and I know I'd had.

Then he grabbed me by both shoulders and held me at stiff arms' length hard. I could feel his fingers feeling my shoulders, up and down all his different fingers digging into my flesh a bit. "Sargent Devereaux" he said, "Our Glorious Cause needs every soul. Wherever we're bound past these earthly years, we're needed now here.

Right here, right now. Every last one of us." And then he kept on me with the preacher look but without the smile. He was grave now, and I wondered why he was worried about where we're bound past this life.

I returned his gaze until I shrank. He's such a distinguished officer, and a statesmen, not to mention such a marvelous dresser, and I smelled his jasmine pomade I noticed that my eyes were crossing on the one flame in the oil lamp. I was so drunk that there were two flames in the oil lamp no matter how I tried to narrow my eyes, and then, after much throat-clearing, I think I said "Sir, I'm not a Sargent, I'm a Private."

"NOT ANYMORE YOU'RE NOT A PRIVATE, Devereax! You're a Captain now!" he thundered. As I stood there stunned, he pulled out his sword out of its sash and swung it around our heads, barely missing the tent roof. "To arms, Captain! To arms!"

"Hip Hip Hooray" I think I said, and then I said something like "Jolly Ho!" with a clenched fist, or something insipid like that. I'm really not sure what I said, actually, but it was something akin to such stupidity as that.

He kept his arms on my shoulder for a second, then he relaxed and stood up straight and smiled a bit. "Care for some more brandy, Captain?" I thought he was talking to someone else for a second when he said 'captain'. I'm still hardly used to it.

"I don't think I'd better sir," I said then added somewhat stupidly "the tent is spinning." It was, too.

"Perhaps a walk in the night woods might freshen you up before bedtime?" he suggested.

I think what I said was "Sir I am honored by your company at any time but I feel I should take this information back to my new recruits immediately . . . sir."

He smiled at me with his hands behind his back and then he put one hand out on my shoulder again, with a little sigh.

"Very well then, Captain Devereaux!" he hollared like brandy makes military men do (believe me I know, you'd be plainly scandalized how many men are liquored-up when the bullets and cannonballs fly and I wouldn't blame you but, having been there, I don't blame them either. Sister, I think in the wake of tasting battle and your recent endevours we'll just have to redefine the limits of coarseness and what we learn to tolerate in those around us!)

"Congratulations on your new company." he said, "You go find the men and tell them. We'll get on all the paperwork first thing tomorrow. I think you'll be happier with a Captain's pay."

"Sir," I stammered, "are you authorizing a company of NINE MEN?"

"You'll grow, Captain." he said, "We'll get you up to twelve in no time, and then you'll have the same chance Jesus had."

We just looked at each other for a moment longer.

"Dismissed Captain. If you feel you must run off, then go ahead."

"Thank you sir." And I did run off! Once, twice, three times I wheeled around and ran off. The third time I found the door and made it outside, the ground

wheeling to the right and the left up and down in the air like a ship toss'd on the waves.

On the way back to my tent I straightened up a bit. I couldn't believe this was happening to me! A Captain all of a sudden, with a company, a very small one, a very odd one, but a military company no doubt. Could they handle weapons? Could they march? My mind spun with it all and the brandy burned off of me as I got back to the lads and I was mad with the news, hollering and jabbering and then suddenly remembering I was a Captain now (a damned drunk one) and an authority figure so I stopped yammering and let the others do it for me. We all talked and commiserated around our tents later that night, long past taps. Warren, one of the nurses and mad for fashion, was sketching our uniforms. Jonathan was bandying about the lavender drapery fabric he'd liberated a bolt of. Everyone was SO excited!

I mustered the men in as privates in the Confederate Army two days ago, with me as Captain and Jonathan as Staff Corporal! I never in a million years thought Col. Montgomery would approve of Jonathan but he agreed to it with that Rev. Baker grin of his, so there you go.

I meet with the Colonel regularly and he is always suggesting a walk together to "talk tactics and strategy", always inviting me back to dinner saying how much enjoyed our little time together. I mean, Elsie, Officers DO NOT fraternize with enlisted Johnnys this way. It is MOST unusual, and yes, I do realize something about what's going on. It's just that I find it more difficult to accept because it's happening directly to me I suppose. I want to believe it is just my fine military bearing that has propelled me suddenly to such heights, and of course Col. Montgomery is most restrained and cordial in all interactions which might drift o'er the transom of any third party, and I don't blame him. He has tintypes of a wife and two small children on his desk.

We have no name for our company, and that's always a big thing. All the men got together over the campfire last night. (There are thirteen of us now! Up from nine in less than a week! Passing up our Saviour already!) One of the lads says he can get the whole bass and tenor section of the community chorus back home to sign up! That'll double us again!

So like I said we were around the campfire and you wouldn't believe the discussion, or the food! I noticed other lads from other outfits sniffing our way at the gorgeous smells. It turns out former nurse turned Private Merrill Simpson is an accomplished cook and even better thief. He stole three eggs from some officer's mess and made a cornbread-sloosh quiche that was a taste of heaven. That and real chicory coffee (cut with peanuts of course, coffee being like gold anymore) and we had ourselves a feast to beat the band and stayed up late into the night talking about what to call the company.

Everyone agrees it has to be a color, but no one can agree on exactly what. Jonathan thinks we should be the Lavender Boys and all wear lavender scarves and half the boys agree and half the boys say (quite rightly) that we'd be driven out of this man's army on a hot rail if we called ourselves that.

Private Spiece (So many new names! Ha!) says we

should be the Beige Brigade because, as he says, "it's obviously the only neutral color that serves all of us equally." he goes on, "Beige will bring out EVERYONE'S eyes! Imagine the glint of our eyes on the battlefield, all of us in blazing beige!"

Personally, I like lavender and beige together. I think it's a nice combination. With Rebel Grey as a base, it's very pleasing to the eye.

I'll write you again soon, I pray for your sanity, dearest sister Elsie.

And I do not want my wartime excitement and involvement in matters here to translate ANY SORT OF notion that I hold your murdering our Stepfamily in anything less than the highest gravity. This is a most serious affair which which occupies what meager time I have to devote to its contemplation.

Much love,
your brother always,

Captain Albert Devereaux

September 15th, 1862

Dear Melanie;

It is your stepbrother Albert. I hope you are well and still at this address in Frankllin. Please give my regards to (your) Aunt Miriam. I am dug in in Virgina for the winter and I write you with the utmost concern. I am privy to military matters which I cannot divuldge, but what I must let you know is it is most dangerous for you to return to Clarksville from Franklin. You should not try to travel on the roads back home. I'm sure everything is fine there, but there are reasons—secrets I hold dear to our Glorious Cause—for which you must not travel. Great danger awaits young ladies! I know we have never been great eggs in the same basket, but I hope you find it in your heart to trust me on this issue.

All the best,
Albert

dear Albert

I am only writing you becawse Ant Merriam says I shuld becawse you ar a soldjer in our Gloryous Cause.

I am verry pist off at you for killing Bart, and you killd him as sure as if you'd shot him in the head. I know how you went on at him in that letter with those fancy words of yours and that WIT AND ALL and you knowed he was too sick to travul and he went and died not 20 miles from his home and its your fawlt as sure as if yu'd shot him your self.

I havn't haerd from Darcy since she left but she can't hardly write anyway and wuld not ask her sister to help her becawse of her pride I'm sure.

But it is herring not at all from Father wich concerns me.

I feer he is ill and yu are in kahuts with your sister to keep us away and to swindel my Father out of his fortune and keep it fer your selfs

I will go to Clarksville specially soon to make sur that dos not hapen and you can not stop me.

Melany

fr: SGT. ALBERT DEVEREAUX, C/O
CONFEDERATE QUARTERMASTER DISPATCH,
ARMY OF NORTHERN VIRGINIA

to: MISS MELANIE JANSCH C/O
CONFEDERATE QUARTERMASTER DISPATCH
FRANKLIN TENN

10:40 AM, 1, OCTOBER, 1862 DEAR
MELANIE STOP I AM NOT JOSHING STOP
NOR AM I HOPING FOR YOUR FATHER'S
MEAGER FORTUNE STOP I AM ONLY
TRYING TO SAVE YOUR LIFE STOP IF YOU
ARE STILL IN FRANKLIN DO NOT LEAVE
STOP FRANKLIN GOOD CLARKSVILLE BAD
STOP SGT. ALBERT DEVEREAUX STOP

TO SGT. ALBERT DEVEREAUX STOP
CONFEDERATE QUARTERMASTER DISPATCH
STOP ARMY OF NORTHERN VIRGINA STOP
ALBERT YOU DONT KNOW TO STOP DO YOU
STOP YOU MUST THINK I AM STUPID STOP
I HAVE FRIENDS SAFE IN CLARKSVILLE
STOP WILL NOT FALL FOR YOUR AND YOUR
SISTER'S EVIL PLAN STOP WILL GO TO
CLARKSVILLE IMMEDIATELY STOP YOU
ARE A FAG AND A SHAME STOP MISS
MELANY JANSCH STOP

fr: PRIVATE ALBERT DEVEREAUX,
UNNANMED NEW BATTLLION 27 C/O
CONFEDERATE QUARTERMASTER DISPATCH,
ARMY OF NORTHERN VIRGINIA

to: MISS MELANIE JANSCH C/O
CONFEDERATE QUARTERMASTER DISPATCH
FRANKLIN TENN

2:25 AM, 5, OCTOBER, 1862 DEAR
MELANIE STOP YOU ARE RIGHT STOP
EVERYTHING YOU SAY IS TRUE STOP I
AM SO ASHAMED STOP MY CONSCIENCE
HAS ME IN AGONY STOP GO TO
CLARKSVILLE IMMEDIATELY TO SAVE
FAMILY FORTUNE STOP

PLEASE GO NOW STOP SGT. ALBERT
DEVEREAUX STOP

Tommy Womack

My Dear Brave Captain!

I trust you are doing well. The papers say both armies have settled down for the winter and I am thankful to the Lord that you have been spared for another Christmas. Of course, I would love to have you home for this holiday (Mother and Father are anxious to see you as well!) but I understand your service to our Glorious Cause and wish you Godspeed in all matters.

I am so proud of you! A Captain! Have you decided on lavender or beige?

We had a thanksgiving dinner at the church and I brought pounds of sausage, which amazed everyone. How did you make such sausage when the Yankees took all our hogs?, they all asked. Is it mutton? Is it venison? It's . . . it's own thing, they all agreed. Yes, I smiled. It definitely is it's own thing. Ha!

The funniest thing happened! You remember old Miss Hancock who had her spinster claws into Stepfather after mother died, the one who batted her eyes at him like they were about to fall off? She was having a piece of sausage and said "I've had this taste in my mouth before." Ha! I about had to hold my breath to not fall about laughing at that one. Yes ma'am you certainly have! Mother laughing so hard in my pocket I' was afraid someone might hear her. I kept pulling my pocket open and whispering "Shhhhh!" in it.

My brother, on to serious matters.

I am disappointed but I suppose I understand why you felt you had to approach Melanie. I can only assume you gave her some sort of warning not to come home, because I recieved a telegram yesterday insisting that she was indeed coming home despite your admonitions not to. I expect her directly.

I suppose I should be grateful in a way because what with the holidays and party season and church and getting ready for winter, I might not have been prepared for anothing killing and butchering without the fair warning.

Still, I feel a little betrayed. I hope you were careful with what you said to her. Murder is a crime. These are serious affairs, you know. It's not just me, it made Mother and Father both VERY ANGRY!

To answer your question of way back, there isn't any "they." Just an expression.

Ah! Speak of the devil! Who should I see coming up the pathway?

Drat! A coach and a footman! Must play nice for a second.

I suppose I'll write you more later. I'm sure I'll have more to tell! (This is like a Harper's story where they leave you hanging until next week. Ha!)

Much love,
Elsie

18, OCT., '62

Tommy Womack

November 20, 1862

My dear grievously insane Sister;

If our dear departed parents are so displeased with me I
suppose I must draw my frosty toes up tight in my tent
and savor the irony of being safer in a war zone than in
my own home.

   I pray all our fellow parishioners and holiday revellers
injest our former loved ones over the holiday season
with a minimum of digestive duress. Having neither met
nor been a cannibal before, I'm only assuming there's a
bit of gastric adjustment, a' la kale.

   I'm of a too foul a temper to write very much right
now. We have a Christmas pageant to put on and I am
neck-deep in rehearsals and costumes and dance steps
and re-writes and ONE THING AFTER
ANOTHER. Will write later.

   Must go practice my piano (!!!)

love,
Albert

Dearest Albert;

I'm so sorry for that what came between us. You know I love you. No matter how angry Mother and Father would get I promise I would always stand up for you to them.

This last killing didn't go so well. Everything's fine now but the stars weren't with me on this one. There was a bit of chasing and screaming and I was a afraid neighbors might hear over at the Farlis farm, but so far so good.

It makes me nervous though. Weeks later I'm still finding telltale specks of this and that here and there around the back of the house where the lion's share of the killing took place, brains all up in the tree limbs for instance. Yesterday I encountered a wrinkled yellow eyeball lodged in a knothole of the big elm behind the root cellar, right at eye level, looking right at me! (That was a start!) There's no way to make sure you've got it all I suppose and what with the cold weather things don't go to rot as fast as you'd sometimes like them to. Oh well.

They say you've always got to be just as careful on your fifteenth murder as your first because one little mistake and. . . .Not really! Ha! Ha! No 'They'! Just kidding! Ha!

Mother and Father send their love and are so proud of their Captain boy. Please have a new tintype made in your Captain's uniform!

A Christmas pageant?!?! Do tell. You playing Piano! Hallelujah! I do so miss your singing voice. Did you sing? If so, what?

If this doesn't get to you until after Christmas, I hope you had a safe and merry one, my darling brother, and if it arrives before the blessed day of Our Lord's birth, I wish you

Tommy Womack

happiest of Season's Greetings, merriest of Yule Tidings and wishes for a safe and victorious, glorious New Year. I have not told Mother and Father about your homosexual ways. There's certain things I'd just care not to discuss with them.

Much love,
Elsie

10, DEC., '62

Dearest Elsie;

Well, now, you've run through the Step Family and I heartily pray this is the end of your murderous road. And thank you so much for pointing out that you would stand up for me should Mother and Father take to whispering nasty things in your ear. That's very sweet of you. For the sake of any neighbors who might rile them I pray you're done with all this as well, and for that matter, for the sake of anyone who might ire that voice of our Dead Mother which ringeth in your head so.

For a moment I was riled when you said you have withheld the secrets of my sexuality to our parents. I was honestly bothered for a second that you would not share my proud and reliev'd state of self-honesty with the two people who created me as much as God did. And then I had to remind myself that our dear parents are DEAD and even if you did share this matter with them they could have no reaction because they are DEAD and whether or not you tell them anything makes not really any serious difference because they are DEAD.

That aside, can it be almost February? Where does the time go? We have had another bad winter in camp with pneumonia, consumption, dysentery, typhoid, all sorts of agonies. We've lost more men to disease than we lost at Shiloh. Men aren't supposed to live out in tents through the Virginia winter, I don't reckon.

But the good news for my company is that we are all alive and well, and we are The Lavender Boys. Yes, the Lavender Boys.

That was Jonathan's title. The rest of the lads weren't

sold and I was quite sure we'd be run out of the army on a rail if we named ourselves such.

Still, I had to admit that Jonathan and Pvt. Betterspaugh both looked smashing in the lavender sword sashes and scraves they'd sewn up themselves, using a bunch of (no doubt thieved) fabric and gold cord and tons of buttons nicked off old uniforms and old patients' clothes and such. I had to admit they looked dashing. Very military, but with just that extra elan'. It helps that both men have legs that go on forever.

And everyone in the outfit has either green or blue-green eyes and, of course, lavender is Heaven with that.

I said look lads, we'll look great, it does compliment Johnny Reb Gray, what we shall do is scarves of one's choice, be it a lavender or a beige if you're a bit shy, and as for a name we'll come up with something a little less fey than THE LAVENDER BOYS OF THE CSA!!! I was sure not even Colonel Montgomery would smile beatifically and go along with idea of a military company known as THE LAVENDER BOYS OF THE CSA!!!

Then Jonathan opened his mouth.

We had a snap mass troop inspection because General Pickett was coming through with a mad preening phalanx of Colonels including our own, and they were snap-reviewing everybody. Now we're not even in Pickett's division. But officers pass through and they do love to inspect anything or anybody anytime. They love a good parade, all of them! Oh Elsie, you've never seen a general so sparkly fine and shiny from head to toe as General George Pickett. His hair's so pretty it makes Colonel Montgomery's look weathered. All the lads agree he looks utterly dashing, though he is a bit short when you get up on him. The lads call him Gorgeous George, quietly of course.

They came alongside us. And were we bedecked out! And very excited! This was our first review from ANY superior officer at all, and it was Pickett of all!

And there we were in front of our tents with everything stowed just so and the coffee pot on the grille and our tents as spick and span and we'd done as much work as we could do landscaping-wise and let me tell you compared to the troops on either side of us you KNEW we were something else. What other company had potpourri steaming in a kettle and fresh cut flowers out in vases for the General to see as he passed by? None, I tell you.

One thing all the nurses had to say when they joined up is that frankly not many troops look very good. That's so. They all expressed the same amazement I'd felt myself but kept private to my breast—that there's just so much ANYONE can do to accentuate one's battlefield appearance, even in the direst circumstance! The right hem, the right stripe, it's so simple. Now there's some dandies already, of course. There's those Scottish dragoon guys over in the 3rd Army and those German mercenaries who dress up a hoot funny, but otherwise . . . us? We suddenly all realized at once, standing at attention, that we stood out from all the other weatherbeaten troops standing at attention. You might go ahead and say we stood out mightily.

It was nothing we'd intended. We just put our uniforms together and all agreed we looked dashing. (A couple of these fellows are natural born tailors.) But I will admit that the lavender, as much as I love what it does for all the men individually, made us a bit of a bump in General Pickett's field of view as he passed by.

We are not many men and the General was passing by at a rather good clip. But our bearing, our lavender sahes, the potpourri, perhaps a whif of some amazing Merrill Simpson sloosh fritters, something caught him. He reared his horse back and slowly backed up a couple of paces.

Pickett looked at us a moment. The Colonels all surrounded him and not a single one of us dared look at him, or them, or anything. We just stared straight ahead so hard we thought maybe we could split a hole in the horizon if we did it hard enough.

"What say you Gentlemen?" General Pickett said.

Colonel Montgomery burst in in that firm but fast voice we hear officers use when they know enlisted men are listening and they don't want us to know how nervous we already know they are. "Sir this is a new company, a recent Call to Arms and still in muster."

"Rather small, ahhn't they?" Pickett drawled magnificently to no one in particular like Generals do. They all talk like the whole world's listening to everything they say all the time.

"Where you boys from, Captain?" he asked me.

"All over, sir."

"Got a name?"

"Sgt. Albert Dever . . ."

"NOT YOU SON! The name of the outfit!" Alas! My cheeks burned and my buttocks tightened. For a second I didn't say anything, and damn it all sometimes around Jonathan Mendelson a second is too much idle time!

"Sir, we are THE LAVENDER BOYS OF CSA!!!"

I shot a quick look at Colonel Montgomery, just enough to move my eyes and move them back, and I could see that Col. Montgomery looked like, if he could dislodge his bottom jaw like a snake, lunge his neck twenty feet forward, swallow Mendelson's entire head with one gulp and bite him clean through at the neck, he'd've done such.

"THE LAVENDER BOYS OF CSA!!!" Pickett roared incredulously, "What in the HELL does a name like THAT say about an outfit?" he asked.

"Just enough, sir." Jonathan answered confidently, eyes dead ahead.

The whole world didn't move while General Pickett thought that one over The birds were rigid at attention in their trees.

Then the General burst out laughing. Loud and hard, throwing his head to the sky.

"Jolly good! 'Just enough!' So it does! Jolly good!" he roared "Very well, kill some Yankees, lads! Let's move along!" He kicked off his horse, laughing again and saying "'Just enough!' Jolly good! So it does!" and the other Colonels were started laughing along with the General and I glimpsed our Colonel easing back into the stern "among officers" version of his Rev. Baker face. And that was that.

So the day after that General Pickett came raging thru camp again hopping mad because someone had bobbed both his horses' tails. Gen. Pickett is a very proud man if I haven't told you already, and he dandies up his horses as much as he does himself, so for the man to have found his favorite chestnut steed stabled and happy but with a tail cut off to nothing, that was quite a slap in the face and he has threatened to shoot the guilty party responsible.

A week after that, posters and handbills appeared all over the trees and posts of this entire immense encampment.

CHRISTMAS PAGEANT
WITH
THE LAVENDER BOYS,
CHRISTMAS EVE NIGHT, 8PM,
CEDAR RIDGE COMMUNITY PLAYHOUSE
SOUTH OF CAMP ON PHIBBS PIKE!
MUSIC! LAUGHS! DANCING
AND DRAMATIC READINGS!
ADMISSION IS FREE!!!

It was all Jonathan's work, and with his typical headlong nature, he'd already decided we were going to have a Christmas pageant, he'd decided when it was to be and when we investigated further it turns out he'd already cast us all in the parts he felt we should play, the songs we should sing and the soliloquies we should deliver and all we needed to do was show up at rehearsals every night after duties and learn our parts.

A week before the show, we had learned all sorts of songs and I discovered to my great delight that the Cedar Ridge Community Playhouse was in possession of a piano!

Now when I sat down and began to play that piano and sing, the miles between us melted. Ahhh, my dear, I warmed to the idea of this pageant more and more as I trilled the keys and the mellow tones escaped from my lungs. I felt like the springs were unwinding inside of me and it was the most liberating experience.

We were set up in the Community Playhouse for dress rehearsal when Jonathan came in with four fine hoopskirts and four marvelous wigs! Wigs! Long beautiful hair sewn into field caps! Long beautiful chestnut hair.

Naturally we all asked Jonathan, where did you steal that stuff? And wigs? There hasn't been a wig from New York or Paris to be seen in the South since the blockade! Why to get a wig one would have to . . . and it all occurred to us at once, what he'd done.

He'd really put us all in a sling this time! "Corporal Mendellson!" I intoned to him sternly in front of the other men, "You will dye all those wigs a color distinctly opposed from their current shade and thusly no longer the exact shade of the missing tails of General Pickett's horses, and that is an order to be carried out immediately this evening!"

"But Captain Devereaux!" he pleaded, returning the courtesy of titles, "This chestnut makes my eyes shine like jewels of the Nile."

"Absolutely not, Corporal!" I thundered, and walked

off, adding over my shoulder "I want those wigs blonde by morning!"

And it was done. For once Jonathan obeyed . God be praised.

Anyway, the wigs were blonde the day of the show, we found some rouge and realized Jonathan's ideal of having a chorus of (quite lovely-looking) "ladies" for a series of joyful numbers, including a bawdy strip tease down to army longhandle skivvies rolled up and bunched up under the skirts. And if it was funny in rehearsal, it was stupendous in performance, with all the hooting and hollering. These soldiers thought they were really looking at girls at first, I think. They sure wanted to believe.

It was a tremendous show and quite a lot of brass was there. Pickett didn't seem to recognize the wigs' origins at all (thank God), Col. Montgomery was beaming and even Bob Lee himself poked his head in the door from the back but he didn't linger so as not to quell the good times going on inside the Playhouse.

And there were some good times! There were many flasks passing up and down the rows and lots of rebel yells and hoots and hollers.

I played piano and Jonathan was decked out as the most gorgeous woman you'll ever see, and most of the fellows who ordinarily hated him didn't recognize him because (a) he was dressed as a woman and (b) he'd newly shaved his moustache off just that day.

He and I sang "Oh Promise Me" from the new stage production of Robin Hood and then the whole chorus joined us for "Buffalo Gals."

Then there was a bawdy sketch or two that had the whole house laughing.

Then Private Winders, another new lad in the company with a lovely speaking voice, came on in a roughly fashioned toga, a garland of leaves around his head and a stern expression upon his countenance. He quieted the place with an upturned hand and declaimed "Friends! Romans! Countrymen! Lend me your ears! I come to bury Ceasar, not to praise him!" He finished a glorious reading of Brutus's funeral oration to thunderous applause.

That was followed by what you would have been most proud of I believe: I started with Beethoven's "Fur Elise" and then into a medley of my best Mozart pieces like you know I like to do. The ovation was a bit of Heaven.

More comedy sketches. Christmas songs. The "girl chorus" singing "Oh Come all Ye Faithful" and all the soldiers in our audience were laughing and enjoying themselves so! I don't think half of them realized that we were the same fellows back in camp whom they usually make so much fun of, threaten to thrash, threaten to do away with, calling us dicksuckers and perverts and they suddenly LOVED us and were laughing at our jokes and applauding our songs.

It was a wonderful evening. And long after the curtain rang down and we were cleaning up. Drunken happy rank soldiers, filled with equal parts homesickness the Christmas spirit, stayed around to chat with my men. It was the first acceptance outside of ourselves any of us in my little company have known.

Tommy Womack

Of course, the more things change the more they stay the same.

Private Smith got beaten up rather badly last night by some fellows who like to act homosexual, lure a fellow into the woods a bit and then beat him senseless! Then three tents had fish guts dumped in front of them one night. Then we've been pelted with rotten vegetables and mud clods while parading on the yard several times. If it weren't for Col. Montgomery's emphatic endorsement of us, I'm afraid we might be run out of camp with pitchforks.

Speaking of the Colonel. He asks me to dinner all the time. About once a week I accept and I do my best to avoid both his brandy and his ever less subtle advances.

He's not unattractive . . . for an older man; it's just that . . . I'm a soldier and want to be treated like one I suppose. He makes me feel cheap, frankly.

Besides, there's a fellow named Henry Meiman in our company that I'm rather attracted to. But of course that's as much a compromise in authority as a romance UP rank would be, I suppose.

I was worried also for the sake of the Commandments and adultery and all that. I mentioned to the Corporal Bailey one day "What about the Colonel's wife and children. I've known the man for months now and I haven't a clue as to who the lovely lady is or who the two lovely young children might be."

Bailey looked at me from above these little spectacles he wears but keeps looking above them so he can see because I think he just thinks the spectacles look nice.

"I doubt he knows who those children are either." he said with a wicked, crooked grin and a raised eyebrow.

We are set to march as soon as the weather breaks. I may get a furlough soon as well! Problem is it's at Colonel Montgomery's invitation.

He says he has a lovely place near Sumter in Charleston. Oysters, champagne and crackers and liqueur and saloons and . . . well, you know. I'm flattered. I'm flustered. I feel like a schoolgirl with a teacher suitor.

Do take care of yourself, give Mother and Father my love seeing as you must insist they exist.

I hope you haven't kill'd again.

Much love,
Captain Albert

Dearest Albert

I have not heard from you in over two months and I fear the worst. We read such awful things in the papers and no one sees an end anywhere. It has turned monstrous and sad, this whole affair and our nation in general.

Mother and Father have gone. They said their work here was done and I was very sorry to see them go. The place is very lonely now without them.

Old Sherriff Parker paid me an interesting call right before Christmas. He'd been relieved of his position almost a year ago and there hadn't been any law in town for months except Yankee martial law. Old Parker went to the Yankee provost, took the loyalty oath and got his old job back, the scoundrel!

He said he'd missed seeing Stepfather at Church and city council meetings and just around here and there and he was checking up on him.

I told him resolutely that one day Stepfather had shouldered his shotgun, saying 'I am going off to fuflfil my son's blessed duty to the Glorious Cause.' and her left. And I hadn't seen him since.

Well do you know what regiment he's in, the Sherriff asked?

No, I do not.

Has he written?

He don't write letters.

Well, madam, he said a little cramped-like, like he was holding his insides funny for a second, if he turns up or sends word, would you please let the community know?

I surely will, I said. And that was that.

Until about a month after New Year's when he came

---

rooting around again with all the same questions he'd had last time, only this time all about Darcy.

I told him Darcy had never been home.

Not since they'd visited their Aunt Miriam in Franklin, he asked? And I could tell he'd done some looking into things, to know that.

No sir, I said. I got a letter saying she was coming and she never did come.

I said I fered what them Yankees mighta dun to her. I thought that was a nice touch. Ha!

And then Providence smiled on me just around then as the Yankees occupied Clarksville once and for all and suddenly this Sheriff was nowhere to be found. I hear he's gone off to join the Cause in Mississippi and we're under Union Marshal Law they call it.

This Union fellow who's sort of the Sherriff now, I seen him from a distance and he's never come to visit or dun anything I know of to make me nervous.

Once a few of Darcy's friends paid a call on the house and they asked some questions and gave me dirty looks but then they always did give me dirty looks anyway, so what of it?

And once one of their mothers at the Parker's store asked me in what sounded like a pointed voice once HOW ARE DARCY AND MELANY real loud like that.

And I said I wish I knew with a sigh and looked toward the North with this glaring look of Southern anger.

You know, brother, I hate to be so deceitful with these people, but I suppose I'm learning how these murders pay dividends in how you have to answer folks' questions the rest of your life.

I can't really tell these people how much Mother and

Tommy Womack

Father had to do with it and if they hadn't wanted it I'd've never raised the first hammer on Step Daddy's head. I at least hope YOU understand that.

God bless you, brother and keep your head down. I don't want to read your name on the agony lists at the dispatch station.

Mother and Father said they'd visit again when you came home. A family Christmas next together maybe! Won't that be wonderful? (They're not mad at you anymore!)

Much love,
Elsie

8, April, 1863

May 2nd, 1863

My Dear Elsie;

So you see there's penalties and I wish you well in dealing with them.

I went home with Col. Montgomery on furlough two weeks ago, and such luxury I've never seen. We ate well, or as well as anybody can eat with the blockades, but well enough (real coffee! Real rum!).

Back in camp there was much teasing and joshing from my lads as they wanted to know all the details.

And they ask me such questions about the Colonel like is he nice? What did we do?

And I say well, we toured the town and saw the gallery, and they laugh and say NO, what did you DO? And much hilarity ensues.

But such comfort is in short supply as I write to you.

For days now I have not been able to put pen to paper yet as everything has been wet wet wet. It has been all we can do to keep the powder dry and see far enough through the rain to make use of our scouts.

Have you ever walked three solid days in unceasing rain? Slept in it? It brings a new perception to things.

After a while you accept the rain and you don't feel it anymore. After a day your eyes don't bat at it anymore. Full drops hit your face and it means nothing except that you are of the earth and part of it.

Of course, some men don't ever relax about it and this tension manifests itself in consumption. You can see it coming—the cough on one day that becomes a hack the next day and then the stooped walk and the gray pallor and you know to pray for them for God holds them in the balance at that moment, and I think it's often enough because the lad keepings trying to think dry thoughts in a wet world. You can't think dry thoughts in a wet world.

And by the by, we are in Maryland now! I never dreamed I'd be in Maryland for any reason.

We are advancing and Bob Lee has grand ideas. I see his plan. The Col. And I talked about it at length one night over brandy and cigars. (I've grown to like cigars!)

We are to strike the heart of the industrial north and either replenish our arsenals, pantries and coffers with the foundries and manufactories up there to be found, or we are to force a truce and win our independence.

Brilliant!

Either way we win, right?

But we certainly are tired. Marching for days on end was exhausting enough as a Private but when one is a Captain and has to keep up a bit more of a front and shout and things, it's even more tiring.

One becomes part of ones clothes when it rains and everything is water, everything is cold.

That's the big worry. When you start to feel to cold. The chill. It can be sweltering hot and you still feel the chill. Boys worry about feeling that because they see that's one of the first signs that steals their friends away.

It is my dearest wish that we push this campaign through the summer and resolve all the countrys' differences so I may return to Clarksville and deal with the havoc you've raised.

A very nice thing I forgot to mention happened today.

We were marching past some wounded on a wet pallet under a tree and they started applauding us.

How do you know us and why do you applaud, stout fellows, we asked?

We saw your Christmas show, they said! Very nice! Very nice!

Love,
Albert

Dearest Albert;

Your letter of January made me worry so. I hope you are dry and the chill has not seeped into you. You always were such a delicate child. I remember how you coughed that winter with the consumption and I worried how it might affect your singing voice. But you came through that all right.

I came across a friend of yours, Mr. Jared. He's still teaching piano lessons supposedly but no one has the money to go and he gets a lot of snippy looks and titters because he's about the only man in town of his age and health who has not been in uniform. Of course, he's so fey that no one would take him. (Do you want him? Ha!) He says he tried to muster once but they told him to get lost. I don't believe him personally. If you're a Flamingo, Mr. Jared is a cloud with feet.

I'm so surprised (and not a little proud) that you've gone as far in the army as you've gone without denying your own deviance from God's way.

Why I bring him up is he says he knows what happened between you and Stepfather that last day.

He says you were leaving piano lesson and Stepfather encountered you on the street outside Mr. Jared's house and accused you both of all manner of vile and perverse activities, saying things like "What are ya'll really doing in that parlor?" . . .

And then Mr. Jared says Stepfather accused you of being no son of his.

And then he says you said "I'd rather be queer than your son!" And Mr. Jared said that stopped the street cold when you said that.

The Lavender Boys and Elsie

And then he says that Stepfather said "You'll never be the man my natural son is."

And then he says you said "I'm twice the man Bartholomew is and you know how I know that?"

And he says Stepfather said no, how would I know that?

And he says thats when then you said "Because I'm leaving town and going off to fight for the Glorious Cause and the medals and accolades and then I will come home and you'll SEE who's the man and who's not and what's a man and what's not."

And then he says you gave him a bunch more earful as Stepfather trotted down the street on his horse but he don't remember what it is you said at all.

I've not heard a peep from Mother or Father for months now and it's very depressing. It's like she's just a tintype again. Nothing there.

Mr. Holland came courting one night. Well, more just visiting but I think courting's what he's got up his sleeve.

You remember him? Well he remembers you!

He says you fought like the dickens at Shiloh and that you were quite a man!

He lost an arm and an eye at Shiloh and is at home now farming and he's much respected in town and I'm flattered by his attentions.

He was a Yankee prisoner for a while but they let him out to feed his family with farm work, best as a one-eyed, one-armed man can plow straight! Ha! I reckon they figured he'd never shoot straight again so why worry about him?

He came to church (with that whole noisy passel of kids!) and we dined on the lawn one Sunday and he went on and on about my casserole dish.

　　　　　　　　　Tommy Womack

It was nothing special. Some beans and year-old crackers really, but he went on and on about it and it was obvious how he was looking at me (with the one eye that works) that he has intentions.

I guess I feel about him like you feel about the Colonel. I'm flattered by the attention but my affections don't stretch much further than that. I guess when you get my age your heart don't flutter like it did when there was new dew on the grass and all love was a fresh thing.

That and those kids! I think those kids might wake up Mother with fresh instructions. Ha!

It seems like ages since I ever sent you anything to the front that got there besides letters and magazines. The berries will be in sometime soon and I'll make you a jam cake and say a special prayer that it makes it to you.

And now you're a fine Captain and you don't have to eat it all at once. Men have to respect you now, even with your perversion.

And I want you to know that I love you in spite of all your non-Christian ways of loving.

I trust this is God's way of preparing you in some special way to be an even better husband and father someday than you would have been, a more sensitive one, when you finally wake up and come around and find the woman who will arouse the true feelings of love in your life like you think you feel for these other grievously confused men under your care.

Well there are beans to pick. Many many!

Starving soldiers often come through the fields and pick beans and eat them raw. I let them. I've had loads of ragged-looking Johnnies sleeping on the porch under the eave and then just moving on through the countryside, going around

---

the towns, headed back home wherever that is. Deserters I reckon. They eat their fill and move on. Some are polite, some aren't. As to their stories and shames, I don't ask and they don't tell.

Supposedly we are occupied by Yankees but they come and go out here outside of town. There's no real law anymore. (Thank goodness! Ha!)

I pray you are well, my brother. Do fight well and strong and come home to me.

Your loving sister;
Elsie

22, MAY, '63

June 21st, 1863

Dear Elsie;

For the last time, if you cannot accept me as I am, just don't bring it up anymore. I know my Bible and, having seen the fellow next to me lose his head from a flying cannonball, I know something of the meaning of true abomination as well.

What I feel in my heart, the heart that God created, I know for higher truth without question.

What I am as a soldier and creation of God is no deviance, no perversion, it is me.

I am attracted to men. A man's face makes me happy. I like a man's body. A woman's body makes me think how her dress would look better with fringe or the right coloring, or that her hair could be better, or of course shoes.

I am a Captain in a fine corps, I lead a company and I am a tested man. THESE are tested men. There is no "perversion" that grips us.

We are soldiers. We have no intramural courting. We are here to fight. We are not crazed animals who "suck" each other. We are men who happen to look great in lavender, raring to strike fear into Yankees and have the last questions on bloody Northern lips always be "who was that man in lavender who slew me?"

Bob Lee's genius is going right according to plan. We are in Pennsylvania now! Of all places! We've taken the fight to them, we have. As the lads like to say to the locals as we march by, "how do you like THIS way of our coming back into the Union?!"

We're just north of a little town called Gettysburg and we have spies saying Union troops are SOUTH of us!

If true, with our great columns, we'll encircle them and squeeze them like we did to Hooker at Chancellorsville. It will be glorious!

There is great excitement in camp! Scouts are coming back with reports of great Yankee hordes! That's a word that doesn't get bandied too much around here. Hordes!

This may be the big show. Pray for me, dear sister, as I pray you come to accept who I am as a glorious creation of God, as I pray the demons of your mind no longer erupt, for the welfare of whoever may wander across the property whenever Mother chooses to speak up again. I pray you see that God's holy law probably seeks heavier penance for the killing, grinding and serving of Step-relatives as it does for the love one good MAN feels for another good MAN.

Love,
Albert

July 2nd, 1863

Dearest Darling Sister Elsie;

I write you with trembling fingers at the end of the awfullest day I've ever liv'd.

My company is in shambles now. Tatters. The Lavender Boys fought heroically. Still! We are in tatters!

We held fast in a thicket and shot over great boulders as wave after wave of blue-suited shouting madmen came at us. Load and shoot, load and shoot, load and shoot! As long as the sun was in the sky, that's what we did, 'til our faces were black with smoke, our lips stained with biting off power bags, our hair in sweaty rings across our faces, our companions thrashed upon the ground in either agony or death's icy clutch.

When eternity had finally passed by, I staggered back behind the lines. I saw Jonathan's lifeless happy face, his mischeivous grin gone rigid and dirty, his fist clenched forward into torn grass and dirt. I saw Private Simpson, a cook to make you forget Wenna, lying face-up and dead, eyes open, brow raised, questioning, like a baby.

And then under a tree, lying in the arms of Corporal Bailey, our Colonel Montgomery.

His magnificent Gray uniform was insulted with a spiky large spot of maroon just above the heart. The cloth was flayed and a little red pulse of blood ebbed from it. His face was the pallor just moments from Grace when there is no pain anymore.

I approached him fighting back emotion. He reached up with a hand and clasped mine weakly, smiling that wan preacher's face again. "Look after them well, Captain. It's a pleasure to have known you." And then he died.

Within an hour of our beloved Colonel's passing, the Lavender Boys were reassigned.

I'd been back at my tent, drinking a cup of peanut coffee and smoking a shit cigar, when the brand new Colonel—Reeder—approached me. "Captain, your 'Lavender Boys'", he spat like a bad drink of water, "have been reassigned. Report to General Pickett for orders immediately."

I went to the command post and it's true. All of us who are left, 21 of us, must shoulder up and march, at 11PM! We're to move two miles north and join Pickett's division!

Queer and odd is all I can say.

Ours is not to question why. Ours is but to do and die.

If I never write to you again, dear, remember that I love you and try not to kill anymore. The killing I've been doing is not better than yours and I make not a claim to it, but I do claim that the love I've felt in this camp and for these men is as good as any love as ever been brew'd.

All my love,
Albert

My dearest Albert;

It is the early morning and Mother woke me singing "Angels We Have Heard on High" at the top of her lungs, which struck me as odd both as she's been gone awhile and also as it's nowhere near Christmas.

She says she expects to see you today, and that I'll not see you in this world hereafter. We're not to meet until the Sweet By and By. I am filled with sorrow but also pride at your service of our Glorious Cause.

I wish I were there to kiss your brow and comfort you. I love you always.

All the jerky is dried. I'm sending all recent Johnny Reb deserters off with a packet of it and they all say it's mighty tasty and most unusual. Ha! "Got a brand name for this stuff?", one of them asked. "Darcy", I said before I could stop myself. And it's true! Melanie won't make good jerky for another three months and that's if I can find some pepper. (Shortages!)

So I shan't see you again. You've been a wonderful brother, and a great man, and just the man God made you to be. I'm sorry to ever give you cause to doubt my love for you, just how you are. Mother says to love you as you are and to stop question things I don't understand. I said I thought I understood full well. She says I don't.

I love you, I love you, I love you and I will miss you the rest of my days.

Elsie

3, JULY, in the year of OUR LORD 18and63

July 3rd, 1863

My dear sister Elsie;

Just a quick note with which I hope to say goodbye to you and I hope they find it on my body. I'm going to die soon.

I am among General Pickett's entire division in ranks just outside a thicket of woods. Our cannon are lobbing shot at a far ridge over an expanse of open field, and we are expected to march defenseless over that field in minutes, and take that far ridge yonder.

As one Reb I've never seen before next to me says "There ain't no fuckin' way."

I'm sorry to use such language. But I can look out of these woods and see the cannon massed on the far hillside and it's true. There ain't no fuckin' way.

I see it now. We are to be gotten rid of.

The Lavender Boys will perish on the field of glory today and there'll be no hometown folks to mourn us, no banners, no memorial to our unique accomplishments.

You'll never know we were ever in this great army. They'll expunge us from the records and I cannot help but wonder . . . is this whole grand disaster, this whole debacle in the making, this bloodbath, is it no more than part of a grander design to purge . . . us?

Would the brass sacrifice an entire General's divison to get rid of a couple dozen embarrassing men who fight valiantly and simply want to be the men whom Almighty God made them to be?

Tommy Womack

Would Bob Lee sacrifice an entire division just to do that? Does he know? Is it all just fate?

I do not know.

Bugles are blowing. I must march. This is the last you will ever hear from me.

Tell everyone I died like a soldier. A handsome brave soldier who looked great in lavender. I'll taste your jam cake in heaven.

All my love,
your brother
Captain Albert Devereaux

From the Headquarters of
General George C. Pickett
Army of Northern Virginia
Confederate States of America

July 11, 1863

Dear Miss Devereaux;

It is with profound sadness that I
return these personal effects of your
brother Cpt. Devereax to you. He fought
bravely at Gettysburg and while it is
impracticable to send his mortal remains
back at this time, we have endeavoured to
send all his material wealth back to you.
Included are many letters. Due to the
immense casualties, military censorship
is impossible at this time, so I caution
you to read with wariness anything he may
say, as the cruelties of war are nothing
for delicate womens' eyes.

With Profound Sympathy,

Major Charles Edward Beauregard II
Adjutant to Gen. Pickett
Enclosure

OBITUARIES

MARY ELSIE DEVEREAUX HOLLAND, 78, of Crofton, Kentucky, formerly of Clarksville, died Wednesday evening at home after a lengthy illness.

She is the widow of Raymond Holland (1839–1888) and is survived by one daughter, Catherine Sweeney of Clarksville, and one son Albert Devereaux Holland, of Hopkinsville, Kentucky.

She was the Step Mother to seven children, John Holland (deceased), Jeremy Holland (deceased), Nancy Holland Rose of Kansas City, Missouri, Stephen Holland (deceased), Anne Holland (deceased) Rosalie Holland Matheson of Vincennes, Indiana and Thomas Holland (deceased.)

Funeral services are 2PM Saturday at Belle-Whitfield Funeral Home with interment immediately following next to her beloved husband at Clarksville Church of Christ on 411 Wesley Road.

She was a member of the Daughters of the Confederacy and belonged to the First Church of Christ in Clarksville.

The First Church of Christ wishes to thank and recognize Mrs. Holland for her award-winning achievements in forty successful years as editor of their annual holiday cookbook.

About the Author

Tommy Womack's first book, *Cheese Chronicles: The True Story of a Rock and Roll Band You've Never Heard Of*, has become a cult classic since it was first published in 1995. It is considered required reading by countless musicians who have passed dog-eared copies back and forth in vans and tour buses worldwide. Womack is a two-time winner of the *Nashville Scene* "Best Song" award. His most recent CD recording, *There, I Said It!*, won a place on the 2007 year-end best of lists of *USA Today* and *No Depression* magazine, among many other media outlets and blogs. He has also recorded with the indie bands Government Cheese, the bis-quits, and Daddy. He lives in Nashville, Tennessee, with his wife Beth and son Nathan. *The Lavender Boys and Elsie* is his first novel.

Please visit the author at
www.tommywomack.com
www.myspace.com/tommywomack

PRAISE FOR
CHEESE CHRONICLES:
The True Story of a Rock and Roll Band You've Never Heard Of

"*Cheese Chronicles* is the best book I've ever read about a life in rock 'n' roll, and I've read it 18 times."
—Peter Cooper, *The Tennessean*

"Womack documents rock and roll the same way Hunter Thompson wrote about politics: raging, insane and full of awe."
—James Mann, *Ink19 Magazine*

"*Cheese Chronicles* has become essential training material for anyone even remotely considering a career in regional rock and roll merrymaking."
—Brian Baker, *The Cleveland Scene*

"If you've ever wondered what REALLY goes on in the life of a touring rock and roll band, this book is a must."
—*The Amplifier*, Bowling Green, KY

"It's the best-written book about rock 'n' roll I've ever read in my life. Tommy Womack is one of the geniuses of Nashville."
—Jason Ringenberg
Jason & the Scorchers / Farmer Jason

"Womack's tale of rock & roll woe is the best book about life on the road ever written (sorry Jack Kerouac!)"
—The Rev. Keith A. Gordon,
music journalist & Editor, Alt.Culture.Guide

Also available from Tommy Womack,
music on compact disc and digital download

There, I Said It! (2007)	UPC#775020769724
At The Women's Club (2005)	
Daddy (w/ Will Kimbrough)	UPC#634479165832
Washington, D.C. (2003)	UPC#690403190127
Circus Town (2002)	UPC#669341100628
Stubborn (2000)	UPC#669341100321
Positively Na Na (1998)	UPC#0640469000724

CPSIA information can be obtained
at www.ICGtesting.com
Printed in the USA
LVHW111010190819
628118LV00001B/31/P

9 780981 886701